TANGLED RIBBONS

KIM SMART

POPPI SMART PUBLISHING

For my parents who always believe in me, my children who love me unconditionally, and my grandchildren who inspire me.

CONTENTS

PART I

BERLIN 1938

1

MAY DAY

Through the children's eyes, all was well in hell. The sounds and sights of celebration ringing through the city masked the brewing unrest beneath. A crowd of excited young children from diverse areas of the city gathered in the park. The Maypole, like a magnetic beacon of light, drew the children and their families nearer. Colorful ribbons danced in the breeze, beckoning the children to come play. In the distance, drums, marching bands, soldiers' commands and cheering crowds could be heard as they marched toward the Olympic stadium where Nazi leader Adolph Hitler would address the massive crowd assembled there.

Three young girls of seven and eight danced around the Maypole, their colorful ribbons intertwining. Blissfully ignorant of the anxiety of Berlin's citizens and their own cultural differences, the friends danced and played in celebration of May Day. The promise of warm weather and long summer days of fun lay on the horizon.

Berlin was a mecca for culture and the arts; a showcase of grand historic and modern architecture and progressive transportation. People from across the country were drawn to the city in search of employment in response to the Nazi Party's hopeful messages of prosperity following the dismal Great Depression. Germans banded together to rebuild the economy and rescue those countrymen who had fallen into poverty.

Nazi influence was evident throughout the city. Swastika flags draped the Brandenburg Gate and floated from flagpoles along the boulevard to the Palace in the city centre. Military trucks were prevalent. It was commonplace to encounter perfectly assembled troops, often with photographers directing their formations.

Older children were forced into the Nazi youth organization. For these three young girls, however, life was still a celebration filled with safety at home, in the beautiful parks and on the tree-lined streets. They found inspiration in school, worship, music and the company of each other.

Within minutes, on that fateful May Day, their lives changed forever. A twist of fate, deception and terroristic circumstances clashed against their idyllic lives. The bond of friendship was tested in unspeakable ways. Only many decades later would they know just how strong the bond could be.

2

SARAH'S SPRING JOY

The renewing light of spring came early. Emboldened leaves of the crocus and hyacinth had muscled their way through the dormant chilled soil, stretching and reaching for the warmth of the penetrating sun. Vibrant patches of the delicate blue stars of scilla spread between the trees in the park. A checkered picnic blanket beckoned guests to sit and enjoy the returning warmth.

Sarah loved spring. She took inventory of the new plants and wakening critters, and daily reported her observations to Mama. She was elated to be outside with friends, free of the confining bulky wool coat and gloves that made her skin itch. The bright yellow cotton sweater, knit by Mama for Passover, shielded her from the light chill as she walked to school in the morning. By the afternoon she no longer needed it. Sometimes she forgot it hanging in the classroom in the company of those left behind by classmates who dashed out the schoolhouse door to embrace the warmth of the afternoon.

All winter Sarah had covered the kilometer between school and home as quickly as she could. Now, she dallied with her friends Gertie and Hannah, just long enough to not worry their mamas. They played '*How far may I go?*' as they passed through the trail in the park, heading toward their neighborhood. They took turns being the leader.

Sarah projected her usually sweet voice into one of great authority. "Gertie, take ten kangaroo hops forward."

Gertie, eager to be the first to reach Sarah, hopped twice before Sarah stopped her. She had forgotten the obligatory plea for permission.

"Gertie, you didn't have permission. Go back to the beginning." Gertie performed a dramatic about-face and stomped back to the starting line.

"Hannah, five bunny hops forward," Sarah commanded.

In her melodic voice Hannah responded, "May I?"

"Yes, you may."

The girls imitated monkeys and rabbits, but when it came to the snake, Gertie called the game over and started a game of tag.

Gertie first tagged Hannah, who was easier to catch than Sarah. Sarah's brother Isaac and his friends also enjoyed the freedom from winter gear as they made their way home. Isaac tapped Sarah on the head teasingly as he ran by on the way to play hide and seek through the park. He distracted her just long enough for Hannah to catch and tag her. Some boys picked up branches discarded by the poplar trees in the spring winds and pretended they were soldiers carrying guns.

Isaac's father had forbidden him from playing with pretend guns. "I do not want you to get comfortable pointing a weapon that can bring such destruction to a person and their family so you become cavalier about its power."

Their father seemed to always worry now. Sarah did not understand everything her father had said about playing soldier, but Isaac must have. She never saw him pick up a stick like some boys did. She would tell on Isaac if he did. Sarah followed the rules and thought Isaac should too.

The country's unrest had changed the tone of their childhood games and life in the community. They moved more cautiously along their usual routes. Sarah became vigilant and noticed anything out of place. One day they were walking home from school and encountered a man pulling a cart on the trail. Sarah insisted the girls take a detour through the grass so they did not have to face the stranger.

Gertie, the fearless one, challenged Sarah. "You're just scared that the *butzemann* will pop out of the cart and take you away because you have been a naughty girl."

"That's not true. I have not been naughty."

"Yes, you were. You bought candy on the Sabbath." Gertie laughed, knowing that it was not true but wanting to light a fire in her friend. Even at the young ages of seven and eight, their personalities were clear. Always observant, Gertie subconsciously noted differences amongst them. She knew that Sarah was equally smart and could run as fast as she, but their friend Hannah was kinder and gentler than Gertie would ever be. Sarah was kind too and loved animals. She would never step on a bug or smash a spider. Gertie would do so in an instant.

3

GERTIE THE PROTECTOR

"One more time Papa, please. One more time." Gertie begged her father to swing her and toss her high into the air one last time before they went inside for dinner. Her stomach pulsed as she descended from the air up where the birds fly. Gertie was the happiest three-year-old in her world. Papa, her hero, played with her, protected her from monsters lurking in the shadows of her room at night, and cradled her in his big strong arms when she fell down.

"Just this one last time and then we have to go to dinner. Mama has called us twice already, and it's not nice for us to leave her waiting while we are out here having such fun."

"She can come play with us."

This made Papa laugh and wrap his arms more tightly around Gertie as she landed in his embrace from a free fall. "I'm sure she would like to but right now, we need to go eat."

Life in the Hall residence was idyllic. Papa went to work, and Mama stayed home with Gertie. They baked and played, went shopping and played some more. Gertie liked to play. Her favorite thing of all, though, was stories. She loved when her parents read to her, not just from the picture books but from real books too. The words were fascinating.

With each passing birthday Gertie's precocious nature became more and more apparent. She read at an early age and could recite portions of the liturgy for mass long before she entered grammar school. Her mother was active in the Catholic Church and International Women's League. At five, Gertie started helping with the collection of medical supplies and things to send to children in other parts of the world who were supported by mission efforts of the church.

"I found it Mama. I found New Guinea on the map."

"That's right, my brilliant child. There are children there who have never seen a book and sick children that die because they don't have medicine. That's why what you are doing to help is so very important. Here, please add this to the trunk. Someone in New Guinea needs this more than I do."

Gertie snuggled the silky blue dress donated to the cause. She thought about how selfless Mama was to make such a donation.

"Mama, this is a beautiful dress, and it's so soft. Don't you just love it?"

"Yes Gertie, I do and whoever is so lucky to get it in New Guinea will love it too."

It would be decades before Gertie fully realized the elitist position Mama, along with the others supporting mission efforts, had taken. In the years before the war, they prepared shipments for Samraj, Ruanda-Urundi, Mali, and other faraway places. Each time Gertie looked up the place in the family's big atlas. Gertie and Mama talked about how they imagined life to be in these far-away places where the people had no silverware or refrigerators. At a young age, Gertie did not appreciate the impact that outsiders had in the destruction of native cultures worldwide; cultures that were thriving without the influence of others. But she would later come to that conclusion.

Gertie was content to play alone and spend time with her parents, but when she started school, she discovered the fun of playing with other children. She was outspoken and did not tolerate bullying. At six and seven she had no qualms about taking on the schoolyard bully, often an overweight pre-teen picking on a scrawny, scholarly-looking younger child.

"You leave my friend alone!" She would run up to and kick the shins of the would-be bully. Even if she did not know the young child's name, she felt a duty to protect him or her. Sometimes she became exasperated at the bullied boy who would not get up and run to safety. "If you don't get up now, I will let him have you!"

4

DANCE INTO DECEIT

May Day was a great day to spend with family. Sarah and her brother Isaac were told by their parents that they would not be going to the town's parade or the Maypole dance this year. Instead, they would go on a family picnic near their schul. Mama promised there would be lots of games and cakes for everyone. They would have their own Maypole.

Sarah and Isaac's parents were great teachers for their children. Everything was a life lesson to them, and there were many teaching moments in their daily life. Sarah sometimes grew weary of the daily lessons. Isaac found it an opportunity to challenge his parents as he tried to show them he was smarter than they were. He probably was, for Isaac was very intelligent and read every chance he got.

Sarah's papa, an educator, delivered the May Day explanation along with the day's lesson. He told them that there was an attack on the Jewish people and others in Germany. The Nazi forces had taken some as prisoners and they deported others. The bias against Jews was more and more apparent with signs ordering the public not to buy from Jews and placards prohibiting Jews from entering certain establishments. "Peace for Jewish people is unsteady in our beloved Berlin. Your mother and I decided it is best that we avoid the soldiers marching in the parade tomorrow. We have heard that the soldiers have become wild and savage and Jews are disappearing at their hands."

"Father, I heard those stories are fake and the government just wants us to leave so they can have our house." Isaac did not reveal his source but delivered his statement with such authority that no one challenged him.

"That may be so, Isaac, and we should be so lucky if it's true, but tomorrow we will be in the company of our Jewish friends and avoid the public streets." Mama described the menu, and activities planned for the day. She promised lots of games and cakes.

Even at seven years of age, Sarah felt life changing in dramatic ways. She didn't know what deported meant, but she was sure it wasn't good because Papa looked sad when he said it. Soldiers seemed to be everywhere. The family stayed home more. Sarah had not seen some of her friends and relatives since Chanukah. She heard Mama and Papa talking about Father's brother and his family moving away. Sarah sensed a serious and worrisome tone when her parents described what seemed to Sarah to be disappearances.

Papa, as a music professor and esteemed musician, had access to the latest music. For as long as Sarah could remember, the family danced together in the sitting room. She learned at a very young age to distinguish between musical instruments. These were the times she was most happy. It seemed as if the music muted the sounds of fear, lifted the toxic particles of anxiety, carried off all the worries of her parents and cleansed the world of evil. After breakfast and chores on May Day morning, the family was dancing to the latest Horace Heidt release from the United States: *This Can't Be Love*. Sarah did not understand the words to the music, but she loved the way the notes floated in the air like balletic bubbles. It was a peppy song made for dancing. Sarah danced with Isaac. He was only a year older, but stood a full head taller than she. He took after their father, whose very presence commanded attention when he was in front of a choir or an orchestra.

A strong rap at the door interrupted the music. The dancing halted. Mama grew pale and motioned to the children to sit. Papa stopped the phonograph. He pulled himself up, as tall as he could be. He was a handsome man and that day, like most, wore a dark suit that made him look downright distinguished. His long stride carried him to the door faster than Sarah had hoped. She held her breath as he reached for the handle and swung the door open, masking any hint of worry on his face.

Standing back a pace from the door was Gertie Hall's father. Sarah heard Mama exhale, grateful apparently that there was a familiar face, and no gun aimed in their direction. It was easy to imagine the worst with all the rumors of terror and forceful eviction of Jews in the country. Papa waved Mr. Hall into the home, but he declined and retreated a half-pace from the doorway. They exchange words, then nods. Papa returned to the room, turned the music back on and without making eye contact with anyone in the room resumed the dancing. The rest of the family joined in.

When the record finished playing and the dancing ended, Papa explained the reason for Mr. Hall's visit. He had invited the family to join the Hall family at the neighborhood Maypole dance in the local park. Mr. Hall thought it would be nice for the children to celebrate the day together. Reassured by the personal invitation extended by Mr. Hall, a military official, the family changed their plans. They would join the neighbors for the Maypole dance at the local park. They agreed, however, that they would not go to the parade.

"Papa, why can't we go see the horses? I love to watch the horses in the parade."

Sarah's father scooped up his wispy daughter and twirled

around with her in his arms. "Sarah, the music is much better here with Horace Heidt, and your mama and I dance much better than the horses do. Don't you agree?"

Sarah giggled and snuggled into her father's arms. "Yes Papa, you are the best."

5

PURPLE RIBBON

Hannah bounced into the room and twirled. The full skirt of the new lavender dress smocked by her mother colored the space around like the fallen petals of spiderwort swept by the breeze into a whirling cloud of fun and passion. Wavy flaxen hair lifted from her shoulders and spun an arch around her face as she twirled. She slowed, then stopped and looked up to Mama's delicate face. Deep blue eyes met her own matching pair, reached beyond and caressed her soul.

"Hannah, my precious love, you are so beautiful!" They could have been twins at the same age, both with the same radiant spirit and pure, tranquil demeanor. She smoothed Hannah's hair with her palm as her own mama had done hundreds of time with her. A gesture of affection veiled in utility. "Do you know what we are celebrating today?"

"May Day, Mama. We are celebrating our family. Our mamas and papas and even our baby sisters." Hannah snuggled close to her baby sister Rachel's cherubic face, cradled in their Mama's arms. She raised her eyebrows and her voice as she said "baby sisters." A joyful grin spread across Rachel's face, and her eyes sparkled.

Like Hannah, Rachel was oblivious to the turmoil of the world around them. They knew a calm, peaceful household with marriage partners who loved one another deeply and were honored to become parents with the birth of each daughter.

Hannah was excited for this day. It was Sunday and Papa, a banker who rarely had the luxury of spending daytime hours with the family outside of going to synagogue, would join them. He had to meet someone at the bank early but promised to be home to escort the family to the parade and then the Maypole dance in the neighborhood park.

"Papa!" Hannah screeched with excitement as he walked into the room. She ran to him, and he knelt down to greet her face-to-face.

"You look so pretty Hannah! Mama made you a beautiful dress, didn't she?

"Yes, Papa, she did. Watch this." Hannah twirled again, her dress and hair flying free in the air.

"Now aren't you just a ray of sunshine! Are you ready for the parade? And little Rachel, you have your bonnet on and look like you are ready to go too." Baby Rachel smiled at Papa as he spoke to her. He kissed his wife on the cheek and held out a small package to Hannah. "Here is a little something for you on this very special day."

Hannah kissed Papa on the cheek and with great enthusiasm took the package and unwrapped it. Inside she found a deep purple hair ribbon. "Thank you, Papa! I have my own Maypole ribbon now."

She handed it to Mama who slid it under her hair, bringing the ends up to tie a neat bow on top of her head. Hannah would always love the color purple. It made her feel bright in spirit, confident, and somehow quietly powerful.

"There you are. Our May Day sweetheart! A beautiful bow for a beautiful girl." Mama made final adjustments to the bow and kissed Hannah's cheek lightly while wrapping her in a one-armed embrace.

Hannah pulled on her sweater while Mama placed Rachel into the perambulator and tucked the baby in with a lacy knit blanket as white as pure snow. It was unusually warm for early May, and Rachel would be comfortable with just a light cover. The family strolled up the road toward the parade route near the park.

Groomed hedges lined the street, bringing structure and boundary to this elite neighborhood where German Jewish business owners and the social elite of various backgrounds lived aside German Catholics. The linden trees were fully leafed, shading the walkways. The faint sweet, exotic citrus scent of the black locust lingered in the air from the freshly sprung blossoms. Bishops weed and lavender had awakened from their winter sleep providing green and purple color spots in the open areas along the walk.

Hannah crouched down to take in the floral scent of the young lavender. Next to family, plants and animals were her favorite things. She loved exploring the hillsides for flora and foraging for edible plants with Oma, who lived in the country on a small farm. Recently, Oma left the country to spend time with cousins in some faraway place Hannah never heard of before.

They greeted friends and neighbors along the way and soon found themselves with a mass of people lining the streets for the parade. They watched infantry and tanks, large cold metal artillery guns, and the new field gun with a forty-feet long barrel roll down the road like a river of steel. Officers mounted on horses and decorated dignitaries in cars passed by. The familiar red flags with the black swastikas centered in a white circle snapped in the breeze. Mini Maypoles with red and white streamers were suspended overhead on wires strung across the roadway. They bounced up and down as the streamers danced in the breeze.

Young women waved handkerchiefs as the soldiers passed, garnering a wink or subtle nod from the young men in formation. The soldiers' legs snapped with precision, in sync to the staccato tapping of the snare drums as they advanced along the road. Soldiers in the crowd waved small red flags, symbolizing their solidarity with the marching troops. Small boys stood in rigid stance and threw the Nazi salute to the passing men in uniform. The air was peppered with shouts of unity and worship of the nihilistic leader. "One people, one Reich, one Führer!"

Marching bands played the deceptively carefree and boldly confident Königgrätzer Marsch favored by the Third Reich. Officers on motorcycles with sidecars and on horses moved west toward the Reich Chancellery where the Führer himself would acknowledge them. Teen-aged boys hung from streetlamps along the parade route in their Nazi training uniforms. They studied the men marching by, knowing they would one day be joining them on the front lines. Wives and mamas of soldiers, arms laden with flowering stems, tossed them one by one, into the passing formations. In the distance Hannah saw the giant Maypole erected near the Berlin Cathedral.

To Hannah, the world was filled with joy. There were happy faces all around her. She felt the excitement of the parade, but did not sense the anxiety and animosity that lingered in the air and fueled the frantic anticipation. She was unaware of the seriousness of the political and economic disdain for German Jews like her family. She did not know that her freedom and safety were vulnerable. It was just another beautiful spring day in Berlin for Hannah.

They watched the parade for nearly an hour before Hannah grew restless. She wanted to go to the Maypole dance. Friends at school talked about going and she hoped to see them there. Most importantly, she wanted to see the brightly colored ribbons flying from the pole, and the blooming trees and plants for she loved color.

"Papa," Hannah tugged at his jacket. "Can we go to the Maypole now? I'm bored with the soldiers."

"Bored, are you?" He spoke with eyebrows raised, making the sternest appearance he could muster on his usually pleasant face. He stroked his finger tenderly along her jawline, looked to his wife who smiled and nodded. "Well, let's go then."

They backed away from the crowded street and walked toward the park near their home. The usually short walk took about twenty minutes as they weaved through the crowds. Once near, Hannah saw the familiar faces of classmates and friends.

"Papa! Papa! I see Gertie. Can I go by her?" Hannah pointed to the auburn-haired girl waving from across the street. Hannah's parents knew Gertrude Hall. She had been to their home many times to play with Hannah, and her mama had visited Hannah's mama occasionally. They lived several blocks away, but close enough that the girls went to school together. Thankfully, their school was not yet a segregated school.

Hannah raced across the street to meet up with Gertie, who looked especially beautiful in a brilliant yellow dress with a matching spring jacket. Long, thick, curly hair, generally unruly, was restrained in a braid that lay like a mane down her back. When she got within arm's reach, Gertie grabbed Hannah's hand and they ran toward the Maypole. Hannah spotted their friend Sally and her brother Isaac already dancing around the pole. Clarinets, a flute, concertina and several brass instruments filled the air with traditional tunes for the festivities. The playful music was a welcome departure from the rigid marching band music of the parade.

Tomboyish and fearless by nature, Gertie pushed her way into the dancing circles, grabbed the first two free ribbons she spotted and pulled Hannah into the dance as the other dancers moved by. Gertie took the ribbon on the inside of the pole, handing Hannah the ribbon on the outside so they were dancing in opposite directions. They skipped around the center pole. The outside dancers went first, twice around the pole, then stopped as the inside dancers skipped in the opposite direction, twice around the pole. After each group had about ten turns, the younger children let go of the ribbons and the older children took the reins. Their dances were much more elaborate and confused Hannah and Gertie, who were too impatient to study the older dancers. They were eager to play with their friends.

They joined Sally and Isaac in an exploration of the park. They played tag and hide-and-seek until it was time to dance again. The sun shone brightly down on them, and the few clouds in the sky were passing pillows that posed no threat. Hannah stopped to study the plants that not long before were blanketed in snow. They chased squirrels, who outran them to the safety of the trees. The mamas had packed lunches. After several more turns dancing around the Maypole, the children joined their own families for picnic lunches. Hannah was enjoying her family picnic so much that she failed to notice that first Gertie and her family, then Sally and her family, had left the park.

6

SPRING SHADOWS

The sun was high. The park was alive with parents and children. The adults grouped together, sharing greetings and smiles. Picnic blankets, bicycles, and prams dotted the grounds. As they entered the park, the musicians announced the start of the dance and the instruments played. The concertina player bobbed and shuffled as he beckoned to the children to join in. Sarah and Isaac rushed toward the pole to be in the first dance. Sarah reached for a pink ribbon while Isaac waited for a green one. Uninhibited, they danced with the other children, some of whom they recognized from school or their neighborhood.

Standing back from the dancers in the shadow of a tree, Papa stood tall and stiff with arms crossed while he scanned the park. He was uneasy and on guard. His gaze frequently landed on his children and on his wife, who was setting up the picnic lunch on the grass nearby.

The first dance segment ended, and the audience applauded. The dancers stepped out and allowed a new group to catch the ribbons waving from the tall pole. They traded places over and over again in this fashion, allowing all the children who wanted to take part to have a turn. Sarah and Isaac played with their friends between their turns at dancing.

"Sarah! Isaac! Come join Papa and I for lunch."

The children had just finished another dance, and the musicians were taking a break. A photographer asked the children to hold their ribbons for just a moment and motioned for the small band to move in. Sarah, Gertie and Hannah moved close to one another and Isaac stood nearby. The photographer snapped a picture. Sarah dropped the ribbon and ran toward Mama. The picnic basket was unpacked, and Mama laid a spread out: tins of salad and fruit, cheese and plates with sandwiches.

"We should have a picnic every day. This is fantastic." Isaac reached for yet another sandwich as he washed down a bite of salad with tea.

Father stood near the edge of the blanket. His smile strained as he watched the other families. Periodically he looked over his shoulder and turned toward movement behind him. "Your mother packs a bountiful picnic basket. She has never disappointed me with her picnics. Well, she has never disappointed me ever!"

His strained smile relaxed momentarily as he exchanged glances with his wife. She reached into the basket and pulled out yet another plate of food. "Today you will really be happy with me. I have here for you one cake each plus a spare to share."

"Oh Mama, they are beautiful and my favorite!" Sarah snatched a cake from the plate before Isaac could grab a second one.

"Here, dear. Here is a cake for you too." Before their father could reach for the cake, he caught sight of Mr. Hall, who was walking away from the festivities with a quickened pace. His young daughter Gertrude turned to wave to her friends, but Mr. Hall reached over and squared her shoulders to the direction they were traveling.

It alarmed Papa that Mr. Hall had not contacted his family since their arrival at the park and appeared to be leaving in a pressured manner. "Children, we must go. Quickly! Help Mama pack up."

He leaned over to help his wife up from the blanket. With the blanket thrown over his shoulder and loose dishes clanging in the basket from the untidy packing, the family started on the path home. Sarah and Isaac were reluctant to leave, but obeyed their father.

"Papa, that was fun. I am glad we got to come. Why do we have to leave now? The band was just taking a break."

"Well, Sarah, I didn't think that band was so good. The squeaking of the clarinet makes me think of frogs living under Glienicke Bridge."

Sarah's mother couldn't help but snicker a bit. "Ever the critic, you are."

"That's my job. Now come along, we are going to take a drive."

Within the hour the family left the city, using back streets to avoid roadblocks and foot soldiers. They were silent as the car snuck out of the city. After watching the growing military presence in Berlin, hearing about the disappearance of friends and family, and reading the world news stories, Papa expected this day and prepared for it.

Rabbi Epstein had put him in touch with a German businessman who was a Jewish sympathizer. Sarah's father provided the businessman with family photographs and signatures, ages and names so he could prepare false documents for the family. When the documents were returned, each family member had a new name and place of birth. Their birthdates were changed by one day, one month, and one year. There were baptism testimonials for the children on aged paper. Creases and stamps marked the documents, adding to their authentic appearance.

Mama gave each child their own papers, fearing they

would be separated at some point. Mama had made a little fabric pouch to hold the papers and suspended it on a string for Sarah to wear around her neck. Isaac studied his papers before he tucked them in his jacket. The journey ahead of them lay in darkness. Mama did not know what to expect. Fear rose from her stomach and left a bitter taste in her mouth. She wanted to retch, but knew that for the sake of the children she needed to maintain composure. Panic would help nothing. "So this is how the resurrection works. You go to bed one night as a Fischel and in the morning you wake up with a new birthday, born in a different country and now are a Fischer. Isn't it amazing!"

Sarah looked at her papers. She was not sure that Sally was a good name for her, and she knew that she did not look nine years old. She practiced holding herself upright and making her face look more serious, hoping nobody would guess her real age.

The Berlin music community knew and respected Papa. He knew the primary organist for the Berlin Cathedral and other churches in the city. It was through these connections that he learned of sympathizers outside the city who would take his family in and help them move from shelter to shelter until they could get out of the country to safety.

The family laughed. This would be the last time they joked about any resurrection. This was not like their family trips to the shore or the countryside. The carefree days when they could travel freely through the country were over. Fear and caution floated into the car through the windows, the vents, and the doorframes. They held their breath without realizing it. The waving limb of a tree along the roadside startled them. A cloud blocking the sun's rays ignited a sense of doom. The renewing light of spring had come early, but darkness returned abruptly.

7

HANNAH'S DARKNESS

Hannah could not find her friends when she returned to the Maypole. Disappointed, she started walking back towards her parents who were playing with the baby on the picnic blanket. A group of soldiers moved into the area and barricaded the dancers from the picnic lawn where her parents were lounging.

The soldiers bellowed at the children to go stand in line on the road. Being obedient and unsuspecting, Hannah did as she was told. She found herself in a line with about twenty children. Stone-faced soldiers surrounded them. She tried to make eye contact with them, one by one going down the line, but none would look at her.

"Look straight ahead. Do not look behind you." One soldier in particular appeared to be in charge. When she glanced at him, she had a thought he could be someone's papa. She wondered if he spoke like this, so mean, to his own children.

Hannah did as she was told and watched the back of the head of the boy in front of her. He was about eight inches taller than she, and he wore a brown jacket. He was not familiar to Hannah, but if he turned around, she thought she might know him. Under the direction of the soldiers, the single file line moved ahead down the street. When they reached the second crossroad, they made an abrupt turn to the left. In that moment Hannah snuck a glance at her parents. She could see Rachel's pram and Mama holding tightly to the handle with one hand and gesturing with the other toward Hannah. Soldiers blocked her view of Papa. Only then, when she saw the terrified look on her beautiful mama's face, did fear register within.

"Look straight ahead." The shouting soldier was marching beside the boy in front of her. Again, Hannah obeyed. She felt sick to her stomach and her knees wanted to plunge to the pavement, but she walked on, as instructed.

Hannah, the timid one, reaffirmed her gaze to the back of the boy's head in front of her. She did not dare to look toward Mama again. The image of Mama's frightened face pleading with the soldier played over and over in Hannah's mind and gripped something deep in her gut, awakening a level of fear that she had never experienced.

"No crying!" she heard, as tears silently leaked from her eyes.

"Halt!" The children came to an abrupt stop in the road as another soldier, with Hannah's Papa struggling to keep up behind him, approached the soldier leading the group. After a brief and animated conversation, a soldier pulled Hannah from the group. Papa grabbed her by the hand, and they hurried toward home. As they turned the corner to their street, Hannah's purple ribbon flew off. She yanked her hand away to retrace her steps to pick it up.

"Nein, Hannah, kommen." Papa's voice was as strong and stern as she had ever heard him speak. She quickly grasped the edge of the ribbon between two fingers and raced back to grab his hand.

Mama and Rachel had already arrived at the house. They shoved the pram into the shrubs near the front door; the picnic basket lay abandoned in the bed of the pram. They found Mama packing a bag and the baby lying on the bed asleep.

"Hannah, watch the baby, please." Mama raced into the girls' room. Hannah heard the opening and slamming of drawers. Mama returned with an armload of clothes and stuffed them into the bag. She grabbed Hannah's winter coat and a stack of blankets and shoved them into Hannah's arms.

"Auto, Hannah, gehen." Hannah ran with the bulky load to the car and crawled into the back seat. She was scared, emotionally exhausted and confused. She knew it was not the time to ask a bunch of questions. She looked out onto the yard and studied her mother's flowerbed where the spring flowers stood boldly. Clouds moved in front of the sun, casting a shadow on the yard.

Hannah's father had spoken to others and watched the news closely in recent months as more and more families fled Germany. Through his banking contacts, he acquired papers for the family to transition out of the country. He stashed currency for the trip and to use where necessary to bribe the military, as he had done to get Hannah away from the soldiers today. He learned of a matrix of Jewish sympathizers with safe houses where the family could hide along the way. Their journey was about to begin. The family breakfast with prayer and good tidings, events at the synagogue with friends and family, berry picking with Oma, and being tucked in by her loving papa with the summer breeze refreshing the evening air became joys of the past without Hannah's consent.

The darkness that began with the cloud cover on that day of departure deepened over the next weeks, then months, as they inched their way toward a new life. Finally, total darkness fell over Hannah with the loss of everything she knew as safe and familiar.

EARNING GRIT

As the grammar school years progressed, Gertie had a subtle awareness that life was changing. There were few boys left in the classrooms. Uncertainty about school closures, segregation efforts and military invasion left the teachers distracted, anxious and reserved. Young girls took on the domestic responsibilities of child-rearing and meal preparation while their mothers worked as laborers to support the war efforts. Some days there were only three students in the classroom.

Life at home became a distorted reflection of the happy family life they once enjoyed. Papa was gone more, and when he was home, he spent more time in his study. He no longer played with Gertie. He was pleasant and gave her a kiss and hugs every day that he was home. But he seemed to always be studying papers and books and had a distant look in his eye.

Mama's missionary efforts were brought to a standstill by the government, and she struggled to find purpose. She seemed sad and lonely. She started smoking and often by the time Gertie got home from school she had already poured herself a glass of whiskey. They still read stories together in the evening, but now Gertie did the reading to Mama.

Other things changed, too. Mama used to prepare fine meals, even when Papa was gone; but now, their food was repetitive and boring. Mama's friends no longer came to visit. When they went to mass on Sunday, there were fewer and fewer people at the cathedral. Once in a while they would go to the cinema. Gertie's life revolved around going to school, coming home and reading.

With Papa's absence and disengagement and Mama's drinking and apathy, Gertie felt like an orphan with parents. The SS stole her Papa. Papa's absence extinguished Mama's fire. Mama became prone to fits of nerves and took to her bed. Gertie's friends disappeared and school became chaotic. Teachers were sad and worried. School days were shorter, unless the sirens blew. Gertie's escape into books brought solace.

News about the war came and went. Books did not change. They provided the constant that nothing else could. She escaped to far-away lands and dreamt of inventing time machines. When she finished reading all the books in the house, she started writing stories and reading to them in the evening. Mama often fell asleep before she finished the story, the victim of ethers and ethos. Between war and whiskey, Gertie stood alone.

PART II

BEYOND BERLIN – THE EARLY YEARS

HANNAH'S NEW DAWN

annah was exhausted and weak when she arrived at the monastery. She could not understand what the adults around her were saying. Voices were mumbled, and her vision faded in and out. It was dark and dank in the room made of stone. She was sweaty under the wool blanket but was too weak to lift her arms off the bed to throw the covers back and let the cool air sweep across her wet skin.

Hannah could not remember when she last ate. She knew she should be hungry but did not have the strength to lift her head from the pillow to grab the bread placed beside her bed or drink the fresh water poured from the pitcher on the nightstand. The room and everything in it were muted shades of gray. She had lost the ability to see color and to smell. Her bones ached, and there was a constant ringing in her ears.

Sister Marie was assigned to watch over her in those early weeks. Hannah slept for days at a time, waking only to take sips of water from a glass held to her lips by Sister Marie. The third week after her arrival she became acutely feverish and delirious. Drenched in sweat, she mumbled in her sleep. Sister Marie bathed her body to help it cool, dipping the cloth in a basin of water with flower blossoms and other bits of plants floating in it. The scent of ginger and peppermint filled the room. Several vases of wild rose sprigs were placed around the room, adding a sweet, calming scent to the air.

Hannah fell into a deep sleep. Sister Marie continued to keep watch over her, perched on a straight-back wooden chair beside the bed. Occasionally she held Hannah's hand. Other times she prayed, silently and aloud. "Heavenly Father of mercy and comfort, if it is your will, please return this child to health so she may come to know your compassion and goodness. Bring me vision and wisdom, if it is your will, to use the plants and sounds of the earth you have so bountifully provided, to aid in your healing of this child."

Sister Marie's hands moved across Hannah's body, touching first the top of her head, then her forehead, neck, chest, stomach and moving down her body. Occasionally she waved her hands over Hannah's body, as if to brush away an invisible spider web suspended in the air.

Many years later Hannah would recount to Sister Marie a vision she had during this time. A man came to her. He walked up to her and held out a basket of flowers. Hannah could see the vibrant colors of the flowers, each one a different shape. She had never seen most of the varieties of flowers in the basket. There were more than she could count. She gently parted the flowers on the top of the basket to reveal more interesting blossoms beneath. There were twigs with green leaves amongst the flowers. Some looked like single long thin leaves while others had spiny leaves lined orderly along the length of the twig. Yet others looked like mini trees with many tiny green leaves. The man placed his hand softly on the top of her head. He reached down with his thumb and rubbed it lightly across her forehead. "When you choose it, you have the power to heal others. These are your tools." Hannah heard water drops falling softly in the distance. The man faded away, and she saw only the blue of the sky and the green of the grass where he once stood.

Hannah opened her eyes. The room was dark with no windows; a lamp provided a soft light. The light was yellow. She could see color again. Out of the corner of her eye she saw Sister Marie rinsing a cloth in the water bowl. As she squeezed water from the cloth, drops of water fell back into the bowl: plop, plop, plop. Sister Marie turned her kind face to Hannah and smiled. "Hello little sister."

Hannah tried to speak, but her throat was too dry. As Sister Marie turned to pour water from the pitcher, Hannah spotted flowers and green leaves floating in the water basin. An image of the basket of flowers and twigs flashed in her mind. The water was difficult to swallow at first because she was so parched. After a couple of sips, she felt she could speak.

"Erzieher?" Hannah's hoarse voice mustered. Hannah remembered pictures of nuns and saw some visit her friend's house back in Berlin. She recognized the dress, but the hat was a little different; it didn't have wings. Back home she and her friends would say the nuns were angels in dresses because of the winged hats.

"No, my dear," Sister Marie responded in German. "I am not your teacher, at least not in the schoolhouse. I am the overseer of the garden. I tend to the plants and make medicines. I am here to help you get better."

"You put those flowers in the water bowl? They smell like lavender."

"Ah, I see you know your flowers. You are correct. That lavender is to help the sores on your skin and the ache in your bones heal." Sister Marie brought the bowl of water closer for Hannah to see and smell.

"I smell the roses over there but I don't know what those twigs are floating in the water. They look like baby pine trees."

"Yes, they do. That is rosemary. It helps to make your blood and nerves work better. You seem to enjoy plants. Maybe one day we can work together in the garden when you are well. I will go get you some soup and then you can rest more. Soon you will be well and can meet the others and go to the classroom."

Sister Marie was gone just a short while. She returned with a bowl of broth thick with chopped green leaves and a strong odor. Hannah recalled that odor when Mama roasted chicken for Shabbat back in Berlin. "Garlic," her mama used to say, "will keep you warm and full, preserve your beauty, take away bad bugs from your tummy and one day bring you a baby."

Hannah knew she didn't want a baby; she was too young. But maybe bad bugs were causing her to feel sick, so she ate a few bites before turning toward the wall to rest more. She fell asleep thinking about her mother, baby sister and father. She didn't want to ask. Somehow she knew they were gone but asking Sister Marie to say it was more than she could bear at that moment.

When she woke again, Sister Marie was no longer at her side. A change of clothes was draped over the chair and a fresh basin of water was beside the bed. Hannah felt weak, but was strong enough to wash her hands and face and put on the clothes. She had never seen these clothes before, but they smelled fresh. Her old shoes were there too, but they were cleaned and polished. Her purple ribbon lay under the clothes. It was washed and pressed and looked as new as the day Papa gave it to her.

After dressing, Hannah stepped outside the room she had been in for a few weeks. The bright light from the sun caught her by surprise as she opened the door. She squeezed her eyes shut for a few seconds and blinked several times until she could tolerate the light. The room was at one end of a hallway. At the opposite end a large window looked out onto a garden. It was midmorning, and the sunlight illuminated the garden and streamed through the window. Hannah smelled fruit and spices and heard people moving around. She turned down another hallway and found herself in a large room with chunky wooden tables and benches to the left and a large kitchen to the right. One of the Sisters working there saw her, rushed to her side and helped her over to a table near the kitchen. She motioned for her to sit and scurried back to the kitchen. In minutes she returned with a tray overflowing with food. There was stewed fruit and fresh fruit, juice, porridge and a biscuit with butter. The Sister bent down on one knee, touched her head and chest, mumbled something Hannah did not understand, and stood up. She motioned for Hannah to eat. Hannah tried to recall what Mama said before they ate but she couldn't remember which were the right words when cereal and fruit were mixed at the same meal. She spoke the few words she could remember, giving thanks to the King of the Universe, and quickly ate much of the food on the tray. With a full stomach and renewed energy Hannah was eager to explore her new home, albeit at a dawdling pace. She still felt weak and stiff from lying in bed so long. She took the tray of dishes to the kitchen and a woman showed her where to clean them before heading out to explore the garden.

Hannah stepped outside the door and paused. She closed her eyelids; the sunlight illuminated them like curtains the color of ripe peaches. Bone by bone she felt the sun bake life back into her body. She opened her eyes and looked down at her arms and legs. It surprised her to see how thin they had become. Yet her fingers seemed to have gotten longer and her shoes felt tight. When she looked forward, she saw the finest garden she had ever seen.

Her eyes danced from flower to flower, taking in the hues of pink, red, yellow, purple and orange, some unlike any she had ever seen before. The sunny yellow flowers beckoned for attention. She paused for a moment and took in a deep breath. The places in her heart and soul left void from the many recent losses softened to the smells and sights around her. The leaves and blossoms waving in the breeze brought back a sense of life and the slightest smile to her lips. She took in a broader view and discovered that she was standing on the edge of one of many gardens. There were herbs and vegetables, flowers and shrubs. In the distance she could see trees. She explored for a short time but quickly became weak and tired. As she opened the door to the monastery, she caught the scent of fresh mint and lavender. Tired but refreshed, she was ready to learn more about this strange new place she found herself in.

She returned to the room to rest and found that the flowers were changed and the room now smelled of citrus. A fresh peach and a glass of water with a mint leaf sat on the nightstand. She undressed, and put on the clean nightshirt that was laid out for her. She neatly folded the clothes just as she had found them. After eating the peach, drinking the water and washing her hands and face in fresh water that smelled of verbena, she returned to the solace of sleep where her mind could break from the constant worry and wonder of her family.

10

GERTIE'S WAR GRIP

Gertie wore a harsh edge. She no longer freely sought adventure amongst the manicured hedges and color-infused flowerbeds of the once pristine Berlin neighborhood. As a young girl, she thrived on compliments about her beautiful ribbons and dresses and bouncy demeanor. As a teen in war-torn Berlin, she disguised her natural beauty and budding shapeliness beneath masculine attire. She lived life in the shadows, dodging the spotlight whenever possible.

WW II was fully underway. Unlike some of her friends, she could not pretend that everything was normal. Others went about their lives like nothing had changed, escaping to the surrealism offered by cinema or meeting up with friends for shopping and soda. Gertie read newspaper accounts of events across the world and observed as Jews and sympathizers were taken away. Jewish shops closed; doctors, lawyers and tailors disappeared. Beggars appeared in the streets. Her beloved Berlin ceased to bring solace. Air raids lasted hours at a time, usually while she was at school where she sheltered with her classmates. The first few times she worried about her mother's wellbeing. She ran home to check on her as soon as the teachers released the students from the shelter. She found her mother moving around in a half-aware state, oblivious to the raids. On days off from school Gertie snuck around the neighborhoods outside of her own to assess the damage. It always surprised her to find that relatively few people died in the early attacks despite the immense damage to the buildings.

Gertie's father was swallowed up by the war because of his military obligations. He was gone for long periods of time. When he was home, he was not the same happy family man he was before the war. His mood was dark and distant. One of their shared loves, however, never faded. Papa always had at least one new book for her when he returned from his weeks away. In return she presented him with the new stories she had written during his absence. She hoped that reading her stories of adventure would bring him joy. He never said if he enjoyed them, or even read them.

In early 1945 Gertie was 15 years old, yet she had seen a lifetime of loss and destruction. News of concentration camps and the liberation of imprisoned Jews in Poland was being whispered across the country. Soldiers described unimaginable sights. The Third Reich was crumbling, and Berlin's future was uncertain. Gertie's father was dispatched for duty again. Gertie remembered Papa as a handsome, energetic man despite being nearly twenty years her mother's senior. However, since the beginning of the war he had aged well beyond his years. He appeared gaunt and withdrew more than ever. He refused to talk about work or answer questions about news of the concentration camps.

When at home, Papa was withdrawn and exerted no effort to fortify the family home against attack or repair the damage that had already occurred. He suggested that Mama take Gertie to her sister's home on the outskirts of the city, away from the bull'seye the historic center of Berlin had become. Mama was paralyzed with fear and indecision. She held tightly to the remnants of her life in their fractured home.

Gertie's mother had never been an effective disciplinarian,

and Gertie took pleasure in pushing the limits. She stayed out until past curfew. She took money from her mother's purse and bought cigarettes. Initially, she hid them in a tin behind the house but eventually stopped hiding them and smoked whenever she wanted. One day in early March Gertie came home to find Mama crying at the kitchen table. Gertie knew something tragic had happened. For months her mother had been void of feeling, moving through days like an emotional corpse. Gertie could not recall the last time she saw a smile on Mama's once-radiant face.

"Papa has died in an accident," she sobbed. "He was working near Weimar and there was some accident. SS officers were here earlier to tell me he did not survive. They brought these medals and ribbons from his uniform."

Gertie looked down at the objects lying on the table. Cold metal pieces of a father she had lost years before were all that remained besides her memories. A man who had faded away into the rubble of his crumbling beloved Germany.

Gertie wasn't sad. It had been a long time since she felt close to Papa. She didn't feel sad for Mama either. She felt nothing and initially had no thoughts about how their world might change. His death largely went unnoticed, a trivial byproduct of the massive destruction around them.

The army buried Papa's body where he died. The local undertakers, the few who remained in the city, were overwhelmed with the volume of war casualties. The cathedral where the family had attended mass for all of Gertie's life was badly damaged. Mama and Gertie lit a candle for Papa in the cellar of their home and sat in silence to remember him. Gertie knew that they could no longer safely stay in their home and Mama was on the verge of losing what little sanity she still possessed. As the evening darkness settled in two days after the news of her father's death, Gertie knew it was time to move. It was a last-ditch effort to keep her mother from falling into the depths of madness which Gertie suspected hovered close by.

"Mama, pack a bag. We are going to Auntie Silkie's." Gertie spoke firmly as she filled a pillowcase with the food they had in the house.

"Gertie, we cannot! It is not safe to leave the house. We have no protections now that your Papa is gone. You know what they will do to us if the soldiers catch us. It's not safe. No!"

"Fine then, go without a bag." Gertie grabbed her mother by the arm and pulled her out the door to the garage where the car sat, dusty from being parked for months without moving. Gertie held her breath as she turned the key in the ignition. With a screech and a jolt, the engine came to life. The gas gauge was broken, and there was no place to purchase fuel. The garage doors opened into the darkness of night. With dogged determination, Gertie backed the car out slowly to the end of the drive and turned onto the street, heading toward Falkensee. Mama's sister lived there, just fourteen miles to the northwest when the roads were clear and open. They drove with the lights out, inching their way down side streets, hugging the sidewalks. The light of the moon sufficed to keep them from hitting parked cars. One road was blocked with building rubble and downed trees, forcing them to detour. The moment headlights came into view, Gertie turned the engine off and they laid down as low as they could get in the sedan. Mama was silent the entire ride, hands tightly clasped in her lap.

After about two hours, the car sputtered and died. Gertie could not revive the fuel-deprived engine. She reached behind Mama's seat and grabbed the heavy pillowcase. Abandoning the car, they set out to walk the last few miles to Silkie's house. Gertie held her mother's hand to provide comfort and keep her from stumbling and falling in the dark. They crept through the bushes along the Havel river until they found an unguarded crossing across the narrows. Daylight was breaking when they quietly tapped on Silkie's door.

Silkie was widowed before the war. Her only son, a slightly

built boy of 16, joined the army the year prior and was killed just two months into his service. Having lost the family home in the early '40s, Silkie now rented one room on the main floor of a boarding house. She worked as a secretary. Like Mama, she had become an anxious woman whose once peaceful face was lined with worry, aging her far beyond her years. Silkie welcomed her sister and niece and without hesitation gave up the only bed for them to share while she made herself a bed beneath the small kitchen table. There was no sofa in the modest room. "I feel better sleeping under the table, anyway. It adds a layer of protection between me and whatever may fall from the sky."

"Are you hungry?" she asked. "There were no fresh eggs at the market this week so there are only powdered eggs and there is some bread. I have some dried mushrooms that I gathered last fall and some potatoes."

Gertie pulled a sock out of her jacket pocket. "Here, I have all the cash we had in the house and our ration tickets. Auntie Silkie, I can get us extra commodities by running cigarettes. I have contacts in city-centre if I can find a supplier."

"Gertie, no you won't. You stay right here with Silkie and I." Her mother protested more forcefully than Gertie had seen from her in some time.

Within days of their arrival Silkie returned from work with news of Hitler's order to destroy German military communication and transportation facilities. Berlin city-centre was too dangerous for Gertie and her mother to return. Gertie could not stay cooped up in the tiny apartment so she took it upon herself to stand in line for rations and looked for odd jobs for pocket money. The local hang-out near the town market with an old radio blasting news of the war was the village's central life force. Here, Gertie came to know some local youth. From the locals she learned that there was a branch of the Sachsenhausen concentration camp on the outskirts of Falkensee.

"Mama, did you know there is a concentration camp right

here near Falkensee? The kids in town say it's a work camp and there are Jewish prisoners, German sympathizers, Russians, Norwegians and Poles."

"That cannot be true, Gertie. Those kids are telling you lies. You be careful who you talk to."

Later in the day, when Silkie returned from work, Gertie and Mama learned the truth.

"Auntie, I met a girl from town who said her papa makes deliveries for the army to a concentration camp just outside Falkensee. Is it true?"

"Gertie, you be careful who you are talking to. It's very difficult to trust even those who once were your favored friends and best neighbors with all the distrust Hitler has taught us. But, yes, it is true."

"Sister, it isn't true."

"Yes, I'm afraid it is. It's best though if we don't speak of it. We do not want to join them. Please, keep your tongue and do not speak ill of the government. I have heard of villagers disappearing for less."

Gertie took heed of Aunt Silkie's advice and did not talk about the government or political things when she went out for rations. She did not find any work, but scrounged up some old books to read. There were long days to fill, and the books bridged part of the void. She helped her mother with some simple sewing projects. They prepared the meager meals shared with Silkie and kept the apartment clean.

After a month of living in the cramped apartment with Silkie and Mama, Gertie slipped out into the dusky evening for a cigarette. She was walking down the alley behind the market when she heard shouting. Crouching behind some crates at the edge of the alley, she could see out into the street without being seen. Soldiers herded a couple hundred men, women, and children up the street toward the forest outside the village. They wore tattered, oversized clothes, some in striped prison uniforms. Weak and frail, some fell to the ground. Fellow prisoners assisted them to their feet while German soldiers yelled at them to move on. Some tried to run but weakness allowed them only to shuffle up the road. When they had passed and the street was clear, Gertie ran back to the apartment to report what she had seen.

Silkie shared what she knew. "The wife of an SS guard came into the office today. She said the foreign troops are moving closer and Hitler ordered that the concentration camps be evacuated. The prisoners are being set free. They were told not to come into town but to keep going north and west into the forest."

With worry and irritation Gertie protested. "Auntie, the nights are too cold for them. Where will they stay? Who is tending to them? They did not look like they could even stand upright, they are so frail."

"I'm sure the allied troops will provide medical attention to them Gertie. It's not your job to save them. They were imprisoned for a reason and don't you go thinking you can change that."

Gertie embraced herself, arms crossed tightly over her midsection, restraining the burning fury building inside her. "Auntie, it is simply not fair. We don't even know that they did anything wrong to cause them to be in prison. Don't you see that this whole war is a sham? My Jewish friends and their families never did anything wrong, then suddenly they all disappeared. I wonder if they ended up in camps like this and were starved like those prisoners I saw today. They set the prisoners free, but they don't look like they will live to see tomorrow, their first free day under a new morning sun."

"Gertie." Mama intervened. "There are things that we do not know and may never understand. I beg of you, do not get a wild hair and do something rash. If the prisoners are being set free, the war must be nearly over and we will be able to return home. I beg of you, keep your wits about you. If not for me, then for your father's sake. We have already lost so much to this war, I cannot bear the thought of something happening to you too."

"Mama. I hear you. I need you to hear me, too. It is not right what Hitler and the SS are doing. It's tragic and because we Germans are so scared, we are letting bad things happen to very good people. Of course, I will not try to rescue those prisoners I saw today. But I tell you this. If I have bread in my pocket when I see one on the street, I will surely give it to them, even if I must go hungry for a week."

The room fell into silence for the rest of the night. The following day their world changed again.

Gertie was at the market, under the pretense of buying fresh produce, which was rarely available but always desired. She was, instead, hoping to learn more about the release of the prisoners and their welfare. A truck arrived to unload commodities, none of which were the hoped-for fresh produce. The driver said he had passed a medical tent north of town and saw several released prisoners there.

"There were also bodies of those who fell within thirty meters of the tent. They died free but did not have the strength to make it to safety."

Gertie was enraged. She left the market empty-handed and leaned against the side of the building as she smoked a cigarette. A tear escaped from her eye. Irritated, she wiped it away with the back of her hand. How, she wondered, can she help the sick and weary prisoners? The second cigarette provided no answers either and she dragged herself back to the apartment, deep in thought and feeling at a loss. When she arrived at the boarding house, all the tenants were gathered around the radio in the parlor. The announcer just delivered news of Hitler's death.

"Oh, thank God!" one elderly man, blinded by cataracts, shouted as he wiped a tear from his cheek.

"God? Don't you mean thank the allies?" Gertie muttered under her breath.

She followed Mama and Auntie back to their room in silence.

The dinner table was set. They sat down to eat boiled potato and meat stew.

"Gertie, we will be able to go home now."

"Really, Mama. Home to what? Who is in control now? Maybe this is just more propaganda for the Nazi party to weed out the loyalists."

"Oh Gert, why do you always look at things so bleakly? With the Führer gone, Berlin can return to the beautiful city we once knew, full of life and culture."

"Oh Mama, you are such the dreamer. That life... the one with Papa and our Jewish friends, our beautiful cathedral and jobs... that life has disappeared. Berlin is not yet safe. It will be some time until the allies take it over and lay claim to our Berlin. I'm sorry Silkie, but I don't think you can be rid of us yet."

"Oh Gertie, never you mind. I have been so happy for your company these past weeks. I no longer cry myself to sleep at night from fear and loneliness. I know this is no way for you to live, but maybe when the school term starts in the fall, we will move past this and you can resume your studies. You are such a brilliant child. I know this has to be stifling for you living in this one room with two old ladies."

Silkie left the table and opened a small cupboard. She returned to the table with a bottle of homemade wine in her hand. "I've been saving this for a special occasion and I think this is just the one. Drink up your tea and let me pour you a shot."

Gertie and Mama quickly complied, and soon the three felt calm. After the second shot, they were on the verge of giddy.

"Auntie, those grapes had some oomph to them! I feel like I could float away."

"Ha! Grapes, nothing. This is wild strawberry wine, and it's been aging since before I became a widow." They laughed and put themselves to bed for the night.

Over the next several weeks, the trio followed the radio news as reports of heavy bombing in Berlin continued. Finally, in June, the war had ended. Gertie and her mother made plans to return to the city centre, uncertain of what they would find. Gertie proposed she run a scouting mission and return to report on her findings.

Early on Wednesday morning of the fourth week of June 1945, Gertie caught a ride with Frank Kohler, a merchant driving from Falkensee to Berlin with supplies and workers. Berlin was hiring women to clear the rubble from fallen buildings. Frank was making a round-trip that day and agreed to take Gertie in and return her that same evening, giving her time to check on the family home they had left in reasonably good condition just two months before. As he drove, Frank cautioned Gertie about her personal safety as she moved through the streets of Berlin.

"The Soviet soldiers are brutes and you need to avoid them at all costs. Listen closely for their heavy feet as they walk through the streets. Peak around the corner before you turn down the street. There is no end to the unspeakable things they will do to a young woman like yourself if they capture you. If you somehow find yourself in their company, look down. Act ill and maybe they will leave you alone."

Gertie tensed as she listened to the warnings, and the tension grew as they drove into Berlin. She stared in disbelief at the destruction everywhere. No main thoroughfares were passable. Building after building in the government district was in shambles. Apartment buildings were skinned; the private lives of former occupants lay bare for all to see. The Brandenburg Gate, the grand entry point to central Berlin and the linden tree-lined boulevard to the royal City Palace, were severely damaged. Tons of debris made the arched entryways impassable. Gertie was surprised to see people walking on the streets going to and from work and business, seemingly oblivious to the surrounding disarray.

They parked in a field about a mile from the city centre where the women were to work for the day. Gertie's home was nearly a mile beyond the city centre. She passed nobody she recognized on the walk there. Nobody made eye contact. Shoulders drooped, and sadness hung in the air. Several blocks were unrecognizable to Gertie although she had been on these streets hundreds of time. She went two blocks past her home before realizing she had done so. She stood at the end of the block and took inventory. Of the two dozen homes on the street, three had large portions reduced to piles of rubble. About the same number appeared to be entirely intact. The remaining homes, Gertie's included, had signs of invasion with broken windows, doors hanging askew and varying degrees of structural damage.

The door to Gertie's home was ajar. With the sole of her shoe she pushed the door open and stepped inside. There were signs that intruders had entered at some point. Furniture was in disarray, pictures had fallen off the wall and dressers. The icebox was empty. Deep relief swept through Gertie. She could return and tell Mother that they could move back into their home. In the few hours she had, she stuffed rags into the broken windows, wrestled the door back into place, set the furniture into place and swept the thick dust and debris from the floor. The top floor seemed structurally sound. The garage would need some repairs but without a car, it was of little concern to Gertie at the moment.

Gertie was exhausted when the return trip started and it was after dark when she arrived at the boarding house. Silkie and Mama were ready with a hot meal and warm towels and were eager to hear of the status of Berlin and their home.

"Honestly Mama, we are really lucky. We can move back in. It's not perfect, but it's standing. Berlin is not what you remember. It is as if the earth was placed on a skewer and turned so Berlin touched the flames of a campfire in an earth-quake. There is so much damage. So much loss. Our fellow countrymen and women are not nearly so fortunate."

A few days later Gertie and Mama said goodbye to Silkie and returned to Berlin. They spent the summer repairing their home and working with others to clean the debris from the city centre. At the end of summer it was announced that the youth would be allowed to return to their studies for half-days. Where schools were badly damaged, alternative arrangements were made. Students were encouraged to volunteer the rest of their time with restoration efforts.

"Gertie, it's just you and me now. Please, please, don't be a bother. Go to school and make your papa proud."

Gertie's days on the street over the summer had introduced her to a new social element. The black market was booming with the foreign troops looking for commodities and locals eager to restock their pantries and replace house wares. Gertie designed a way to make her own spending money. She ran errands for the women of the neighborhood, previously pampered by spouses who were now missing, deceased, or would not allow them out on the streets for fear they would be harmed.

British and American troops arrived shortly after Gertie and her mother returned to Berlin. The city was divided into sectors with vile battles between the various international troops. Rumors of rape by foreign troops, real or imagined, were pervasive. Gertie solicited a number of clients to buy groceries, escort children to their lessons and take clothing to the tailor. She learned to navigate the streets carefully. Through underground connections she came to know who to trust amongst the allied troops, and who to avoid. She stayed away from the otherwise trusted contacts whenever they were drinking or in a group of soldiers. She was hypervigilant to avoid being followed home or to her customers' homes. More than once she hid in bushes or entered an abandoned house to avoid risky encounters.

Gertie's mother was not suited to the life of a widower. When they returned to Berlin, Mama transformed. She suddenly had energy and life back in her body. Color returned to her cheeks and her long dormant witty humor returned. While working with the rubble crew, she flirted with passing businessmen. Soon, there were male suitors visiting the home in the evenings and on weekends. Mama lost herself in the unspoken quest for a new mate while Gertie developed her own life and friends.

Mama did not notice Gertie's increasing absence from home. By the end of the year, Gertie's mother had remarried and Gertie had a new group of friends. Gertie fell more deeply into books, often reading into the early morning hours. She read every travel book she could find. She became fascinated with various cultures and customs. She studied languages. She even explored cuisines of the world and experimented with recipes. Hers was not an attempt at domesticity, but rather an opportunity to better understand indigenous peoples. By the end of the school year she was promoted a class ahead of her peers and began writing stories she hoped to publish.

While running errands one warm windy day, Gertie picked up a pamphlet hopping in the breeze along the street gutter. She tucked it in her pocket to read later and hurried to the tailor's with a bundle of shirts to be repaired. Later that evening as she washed away the grime and sweat from the wind and heat of the day, she discovered the paper tucked in her pocket. The anti-Nazi pamphlet detailed crimes against Jews perpetrated by Hitler and the Third Reich and showed pictures of mass graves. A knot grew in Gertie's gut at she looked at the paper and thought about all that had happened over the past few years. She knew Germany had been at war but had not realized the heavy domestic assaults perpetrated on fellow

Germans. She recalled the many Jewish families that had moved away, but the brutality described in the photos was more horrific than anything she could have imagined. How could she not see what was happening? In school they learned about the political parties and civil disputes, but she had not before heard of the magnitude of atrocities in concentration camps, mass graves or medical experiments, as described in the pamphlet.

She lay on her bed and recalled the prisoners she saw earlier in the year leaving the concentration camp. How many, she wondered, were still alive? How many had families and homes to return to? She imagined for a moment what her life would have been like if she had been a Jew. She looked around her room. She still had furniture, a comfortable bed and clothing. Some days they had more food than others but she was certainly not starving. Suddenly her body was racked with silent sobs. She ached for the lives that were lost, the families destroyed and new paths that must now be forged. How, she wondered, would a normal life be restored for those who had lost so much?

Gertie started school that fall as the youngest student in a new class. She masqueraded in trousers, and sweaters or oversized flannel shirts. With her long hair cut into a pageboy and wearing no make-up, she befriended the boys in leather jackets and joined them for a smoke before and between classes. She was quick-witted and a top student without applying herself in school, regularly challenging the instructors with hypotheticals and obscure facts. At home, she showed up whenever she wanted, usually just for meals and to sleep. Preoccupied with their new marriage, Gertie's mother and stepfather encouraged her self-sufficiency.

Gertie spent more and more time with friends in the streets. The few friends with intact families invited her home, and she enjoyed the conversation around their dinner tables, learning more about what was going on in the country. At her friend Hermann's house she heard more about the unpopular view of Hitler and the Third Reich's conduct against those they had deemed inferior. Now that he was dead, it became safer to share honest thoughts about the man and his ideology. It was during one of those dinner conversations that she learned there had been a concentration camp near Weimar, called Buchenwald. Her father died near there. She wondered if he knew about Buchenwald, and if he had visited there. He had become so hollow and void of emotion. Could it have been because of the things he saw?

11

HANNAH THE HEALER

Hannah attended classes with the other girls. There were fourteen girls between the ages of seven and fifteen who studied together. When the Sisters took in local children because of illness or death in the family, there were more. Extended family often picked these children up from the monastery later, at their convenience.

Hannah enjoyed her studies and was a good student. She was disciplined and dutiful by nature and rarely required reprimand by the Sisters. She attended mass and prayers, as that was an obligatory part of the ritual at the monastery. A quick study, Hannah learned to recite the words of the prayers, but it was well into adulthood before she came to understand their full meaning. When studying the Bible, she was most taken with the Gospel of Matthew and those stories about human illness and Jesus' healing.

The girls had studies and chores six days each week. On Sunday they attended long masses and sometimes accompanied the Sisters to visit the sick and infirm in nearby villages. They often returned with fresh produce or game from those visits: eggs or smoked meat, a chicken or harvested fruits and vegetables, dried grains and beans. Between their own garden and these gifts, the kitchen was always well stocked. Herbs were plentiful, and the Sisters prepared the food with much love. Some of the Sisters were truly gifted with the ability to bring joy to the table through food.

One day while gathering eggs Hannah noticed that a chicken was lame. Its foot had become tangled in a loose wire from the fence which left a red and angry looking cut with infection brewing. Hannah was twelve at the time and had seen several injured animals. Like the other girls, she helped to feed them and clean their bedding. Unlike the other girls, when Sister Marie got involved in treating a sick or lame animal she quietly observed. Hannah began to recognize the various ointments Sister Marie used by their color and smell. This lame chicken, she thought, needed lavender and chamomile.

Hannah gently took the chicken in her arms. She had seen Sister Marie go into the potting barn in the garden with herbs and flowers in her hand and come out with poultices. Sister Marie had left early that morning to visit a woman having a difficult birth, so she was not around to help the chicken. Holding the chicken carefully, Hannah picked some lavender and chamomile and headed to the shed. She closed the door, set the chicken down on the dirt floor and looked around.

Light flowed in through windows on the east and south walls. Wooden shelves lined another wall above a thick wooden plank countertop. Bundles of dry and drying herbs and roots hung from the ceiling. Baskets of garlic and bulbs rested under the counter and on the shelves. There were spice tins and jars on the windowsills and shelves. Three mortar and pestles of different sizes sat on the table.

Hannah stripped the lavender flowers from the stems and placed them in the smallest mortar along with a few chamomile blossoms. With the pestle she ground them into a paste as the chicken pecked at the ground by her feet. She found a piece of cotton cloth, emptied the paste from the mortar onto the cloth, wiping the mortar and pestle clean as she did so. She spread the poultice on the cloth and tied it around the chicken's foot with twine she found on a shelf.

Hannah returned the chicken to the coup and planned to check on it the following morning. Later that afternoon, however, Sister Marie returned and joined them all at dinner in the dining hall. She stopped by Hannah's table and asked to meet with her at the chicken coup after she was finished with chores. Hannah nodded and felt a flutter in her stomach. She wondered if she had done something wrong with the chicken or upset Sister Marie somehow.

Anxious to see what Sister Marie had to say, Hannah rushed through dinner and chores. By the time she made her way to the chickens Sister Marie was already there, holding the injured chicken. "I returned from tending to Mrs. DuPont's child birthing today and was putting my supplies away when what do you suppose I discovered on the floor of the potting barn but chicken scat."

Hannah's face grew red with embarrassment, and she looked to the ground. She should have taken more care in cleaning up, she thought to herself.

"I came to check on the chickens to see why one of them might have been running free amongst my healing herbs and here I find a chicken with a boot on it. Curious about why there was a boot tied on a chicken, I unwrapped its foot and I see nothing wrong."

Surprised, Hannah looked at Sister Marie and then to the chicken's foot. A smile crept across her face. The foot was no longer infected, and there was barely a sign of the injury she had treated earlier in the day. Her mouth opened to speak, but Sister Marie beat her to it. "Hannah, do you know anything about this chicken?"

"Sister Marie, I am sorry that I did not have the foresight to clean the floor of the potting barn. I really just wanted to help the chicken and get back to my chores. I will clean it up. But Sister, that chicken's foot was cut and infected. You can not see it now, but it was red and oozing with infection earlier."

"How did you know how to fix it Hannah?"

"I have watched you fix lame people and animals, and even me. I remember when I first arrived, and you cared for me. Tell me Sister, I smelled the wild roses in the room and recognized the lavender in the water. You taught me also about the rosemary, but in the water I smelled something else too. I did not know then what I have learned since. I seem to recall the scent of mint and something else, like ginger. But I have not smelled that combination since. What else was in that water?"

"Hannah, you are correct. That was ginger with the mint in the water. You had a very high fever, and I tried many combinations of herbs to bring it down to no avail. That's when I got a message to use ginger with the mint."

"A message Sister? You got a message from whom?"

"Hannah, let's put this chicken to bed and then talk. You did a very fine job healing this lame chicken and I am very impressed with your wisdom to know how to help it."

Hannah and Sister Marie locked the chicken back in the coup and watched as it walked to its straw bed to rest for the night. There was no sign of pain or injury. They made their way to the study where they talked late into the night. Sister Marie explained how she had learned about healing with plants when she first came to the monastery as a young woman. She was sixteen when she arrived, older than Hannah now, and her teacher, Sister Bernadette, was advanced in years. Almost immediately Sister Marie was assigned to Sister Bernadette as an assistant. They attended births and deaths, watched over the garden and other plants on the grounds, and read volumes of books on anatomy, midwifery, botany and homeopathy. Sister Marie kept notes in journals about the patients, and plants used.

"Then one summer I knew I had to go into meditation. I sensed that there was more for me to know, but I would not find it in a book. I went into silence and sat amongst the plants in solitude and prayed for guidance. After three months I received a message that I should re-read my journals and study the attitude of the patient. I had not intentionally written anything about the patient's attitude but I found when I went back to my writings I had included little comments like 'sad, positive, angry, tired, without spirit, peaceful, hopeless, in despair'. I noted that those who were positive or hopeful healed faster that those who were unhappy or did not see goodness in the world around them."

"So you determined that their attitude made a difference in their healing?"

"Yes, Hannah. I believe it does, and since that time I have been more attentive to the spirit of the person. I try to bring them hope and dispel their fear and anger. I have come to understand that it is the person who lets go of pain and sorrow that makes room for healing and joy in their life."

12

HAPPY PLACE

"**N**ow students, I want you all to draw a picture of a time you remember being very happy."

The high school curriculum allowed Sally to choose one elective course and of course, the choice was Art. She seemed to have some of her mother's aptitude for drawing and enjoyed expressing herself in this way. Sally's mother, Rona Fischer, was a gifted artist. By some good fortune, shortly after they arrived in New York, she fell into a position as an illustrator for a publishing company. Children's books became her specialty. She was happy in her work and able to provide adequately for Sally. They no longer lived with Sally's uncle, who married and started a family of his own.

Sally picked up the pencil and sketched out a scene from childhood that made her very happy. The setting was the sitting room of her childhood home in Berlin. She drew the sofa pushed back from the center of the room. She softly drew an outline of Papa, then Mama, facing each other with arms touching as they prepared to waltz around the room. She drew Isaac standing by the phonograph, and she seated on a chair. At the end of the hour as she prepared to close the sketchbook, she looked down. A

59

knot grew in her stomach as she realized what she had done. On a bookshelf behind the chair, she had drawn a menorah.

Sally had not celebrated Jewish holidays or thought about the rituals and teachings experienced in her youth for a very long time. Quickly she reshaped the outline of the menorah into a vase and colored it in with a dark pencil. The focal point of her drawing became a dark vessel, obliterating the image of a once soothing symbol of hope. In that instant Sally's happy place was transformed.

Later that night Sally told her mother about the drawing and about the menorah. "Mama, I remember Papa lighting that menorah and it makes me sad that we don't do that anymore."

"It makes me sad too, Sally. I miss your papa and Isaac. I miss the happy life we once had in Berlin. I remember the good things though and carry them with me. Papa and I, we were very happy together and with you children we were over the moon."

"Mama, why aren't you angry? You never talk about those days and you are never angry about what happened."

"Sally, do you remember the lessons Papa used to teach you kids when we lit the menorah? I know it was a long time ago, but do you remember?"

"I know he talked about the Festival of Lights and the miracle of the oil lamp staying lit even though they were out of oil for a long time. I know there were little presents each night a new candle was lit."

"Yes, the little presents were always a big hit with you kids. But Papa had one very important lesson he liked to teach you, as his papa had taught him. For him, there was another message about light and darkness, and he liked to talk about it during Hanukkah when we lit the menorah. Papa would ask you to remember something you had done to your brother that was not very nice. You were very little then, so the things you had done to him were pretty small. Do you remember anything about that?"

"I do remember that one time I told Papa that I had stolen Isaac's ball. I was so mad at him because all he wanted to do was play with his friends and he never played with me so I stole his ball and hid it under my bed."

"Right! I remember that one. When Papa asked how you felt about that, do you remember what you said?"

"I said that I was happy that he didn't have his ball."

"And when Papa asked you if Isaac played with you after you took his ball, which is what you wanted to happen, do you remember what your answer was?"

"I said that he did not play with me more and I didn't want him to because I was afraid he would make me tell him where his ball was."

"So Papa told you to close your eyes and pretend you never got to see your brother again because he was afraid he would ask you where you put his ball. You were so sad sitting there with your eyes closed. You told Papa that you didn't want to sit there like that anymore, it was too dark."

"I remember that. So, he told me that if I asked Isaac to forgive me for taking his ball I could open my eyes and it would be brighter than ever. And it was. He said I hurt Isaac by taking his ball but it hurt me more because I was the one sitting in the dark and I was the one who had been angry."

"That's right. Your father showed you how to bring light back into your world by forgiving your brother for not playing with you and by asking for forgiveness for taking his ball. You were no longer angry, and neither was he."

"So, you're saying that you don't get angry about what happened and the bad things people did because you don't want to lock yourself in the dark?"

"Yes, I have to forgive to enjoy the freedoms I have and the joy I can have in this life with you and in my work. It's not perfect. It's not what I wanted but it will do me no good to be angry and resentful about what happened, and every time I start to let some bad feeling creep in, I remember your father's lessons. I know Papa would not want us sitting in the darkness with our anger and filling our world with hatred."

"Mama, I love you," Sally declared and then as she looked up to the heavens, "Papa, I love you and all you taught me. I choose to live out of the darkness."

13

COLLEGIATE GERTIE

"Gertie, lovey, on Thursday afternoon could you please stop by the tailor's and pick up my peach evening gown with the beaded roses and bring it home for me?" Sabine glanced at Gertie as she bent to pick her young son up from the floor. Stefan was fascinated with the colorful wooden blocks and toy trucks. They entertained him for long periods of time, which was a great relief to his mother when the nanny was away. Stefan and the nanny had recently returned from their long afternoon stroll in the park, something Sabine insisted upon, rain or shine. The nanny was preparing dinner and Sabine was putting in mommy time, which generally consisted of the occasional exchange of looks and smiles while Stefan played and Sabine visited with a friend or sketched.

On the days she was melancholy and missing her own mother, she would snuggle Stefan in her lap and tell him stories. Sabine told tales of animals in the woods that could talk to one another and play tricks on humans, hiding garden tools or erecting mud statutes of toads and snakes in the garden.

"The mother crow said to the baby crow, 'Oma enjoys

toiling in the garden so she has vegetables to make stew for the children when they come home from school. She is alone all day so wouldn't it be nice if there was someone she could talk to in the garden? Run along and get your friends and we will make her a companion to talk to while she pulls the weeds and waters the carrots and potatoes.' The baby crow flew off and a short while later he returned with his friends; the squirrels and rabbits, raccoons and sparrows. Together they made a big mud toad in the middle of the garden. And what do you think happened to that toad, Stefan? Do you think Oma was happy to see that toad? Well, the next morning after the children left for school, Oma went to work in the garden, but when she saw the big toad in the middle of the garden, she became frightened. She was so scared she could not move. Just then, the baby crow flew over her head and landed on the toad's back. The toad did not move. Oma thought that was very odd that the toad did not move, so she picked up her hoe and carefully walked into the garden. She poked the toad a bit and still it did not move. The little crow and his brothers and sisters in the trees started cackling and laughing, and Oma started laughing too. She was happy to have the toad in the garden and could not wait until the children returned from school so she could trick them with the big toad that didn't move."

Sabine was just three years older than Gertie. She was a delicate beauty with fair hair drawn back from her face in waves, much like Ida Lupino in *Paris in Spring*. She had soft blue eyes and endless long thin legs extending out from fashionable pedal pushers. Glamorous strappy sandals gilded her delicate feet. Gertie would not be caught dead in such a look, but Sabine looked stunning. She understood why the handsome and older Ulrich Wirtz had fallen for Sabine. Mr. Wirtz, a Chancellor's cabinet minister, had a distinguished look with a reputation for being charming and witty. Sabine seemed quite happy in this marriage and with their son, who bore the finest attributes of each of his parents and was sure to be stunning in his own right.

"Sure thing," Gertie snapped back as she raced through the parlor to the front door to make her next delivery. She and Sabine had become friendly over the past year, but Gertie wasn't the chatty type and Sabine knew it. Sabine came from a family of modest means and then married the wealthy Mr. Wirtz after she became pregnant with his child. Their wedding was the talk of the town. The spirit of Berlin, rising from the ash and dust of their crumbled buildings, breathed in renewed life for a new normal as they followed the Wirtz couple. The Wirtz family was a longstanding beacon of possibilities for wealth. The family earned their money through hard work and good fortune. Headlines about the wedding started with pre-engagement rumors and trailed through to the honeymoon. Sabine's beauty radiated in the photos, although she was a commoner. The newspapers reported that she was smart and a natural beauty, but came from a modest area of the city. Young girls, with hope in their eyes and excitement in their voices, were heard saying: "Someday I will have a Wirtz wedding."

Photographs of Sabine in her stunning gown, the ceremony, the happy couple and their post-honeymoon glow sold newspapers for months. They became the new beacon of hope for the city and a nation struggling to re-establish itself. The newspapers, as they will do, exploited the couple with every opportunity they could find or create. Sabine continued to be in the crosshairs of the camera lens and was on guard for opportunist photographers whenever she left the house.

Overshadowed by Sabine's peripheral beauty was her brilliant mind. Sabine and Gertie shared a love of the sciences and often swapped books on physical sciences and psychology. They enjoyed the occasional science fiction they could get their hands on as well. Sabine had thoughts of going to medical school when she was young, but now abandoned such hope. She encouraged Gertie, however, to find a way to get to college. One late afternoon when Gertie made a delivery, Sabine talked her into staying to chat for a short while and share some spirits. The baby was asleep, and Ulrich was out of town on business.

"Why don't you marry yourself one of those handsome G.I.'s and study in the States, Gertie?"

"I'm not keen on the States. I'm more interested in the rustic cultures like those in the Amazon, or deep in Peru. I want to be for the jungle what Freya Stark was for Arabia. I think if I could somehow study in England I would have a better springboard into anthropology field studies."

"Okay then lovey, marry a Brit." They laughed and Sabine refilled their glasses while Gertie lit them each a cigarette. They both knew Gertie was too rugged for a Brit. They liked their women refined and presentable, like Sabine. Gertie did not have many female friends and was enjoying this camaraderie with Sabine.

When Gertie delivered the gown to Sabine on Thursday, she found the door slightly ajar. She stepped into the salon and called to Sabine, but got no response. She climbed the stairs to hang the dress in the closet where it would not get wrinkled. As she reached the top floor, a British officer backed out of Sabine's bedroom, initially unaware of Gertie. Sabine wore only a silk slip, and her hair was mussed up. Gertie turned away, but not before the officer caught her eye. "Ma'am," he nodded politely, and bounded down the stairs.

"Come, come, hang the dress in here." Sabine motioned to her. Gertie entered the bedroom cautiously, surprised by what she had just witnessed. She thought Sabine had lost her wits. "Don't worry hun, I didn't let him go all the way. I just made him feel good about himself. And I did it for you."

"Sabine, don't you be stuffing-up your marriage for me."

Sabine laughed. "I would never! I'm bold, but not stupid! The boy just needed some sweet talking, not my body. Besides, you know how much Ulrich adores Stefan and I. He's not going anywhere."

"Just leave me out of it. Don't say you're doing anything for me."

"But I am Gertie. That man is your ticket to college."

"Sabine, I am not marrying one of those stiffs."

Sabine threw herself on the bed, laughing gleefully. "Here, this should get you an introduction and I can be your blackmail beauty."

She handed Gertie the officer's wallet, opened to a picture of the man and his wife. "The handsome Cameron Vaughan, as you can see, is a family man. His family is also a major contributor to a London University. I believe you have passed your entrance exam, Gert!"

Gertie, not usually one to show heartfelt affection, pulled Sabine off the bed and wrapped her long arms around her in a massive hug. "Sabine, you are the greatest! I will dedicate my first book to you and give you my firstborn; God knows I don't want it."

Gertie was deliriously happy. Sabine was envious but happy for her friend.

14

BOYS, CARS AND THE CONVENT

B oys and cars are two subjects that get little attention at a monastery. But in her teen years Hannah was curious about both. Fortunately, she had opportunities for exploration.

Each Saturday the monastery received deliveries of wine, local produce and dairy to supplement their own harvest. A local farmer and his sons, Ansel and Noël, made the deliveries. The handsome faces and muscular bodies of these teenaged boys did not go unnoticed by the girls of the monastery. The girls all volunteered on Saturdays to help unload the trucks, but ultimately, the Sisters in charge of the kitchen made the chore assignments. Hannah learned later that this was an opportunity for the Sisters to observe the girls in the company of the opposite sex.

Hannah was assigned, just like the other girls, to assist with shuttling the cargo and putting it into the root cellar or the icehouse. She didn't mind it. She liked to look through the produce to see what might be in season that they did not grow themselves. The boys were just workers to her. She hadn't really thought about gender differences until one day, when she was thirteen, the younger boy Ansel, who was few years older, followed her down the steps into the root cellar. They each carried wooden crates of onions and garlic that would be stored and used over the next several months. The monastery gardens did not produce enough to last through the winter.

Once unburdened from their loads, Hannah headed for the wooden stairs to ascend to daylight. Ansel grabbed her by the shoulders. Surprised, she turned to tell him to stop. As she turned, Ansel moved his hand to the back of her head, planted his lips on hers and marked her with a kiss.

"What did you do that for?" Hannah was shocked at what she felt was a curious violation of her person. She could not fathom why a boy would put his salty, sweaty face in hers and his spit on her mouth. She wiped her mouth with the back of her hand.

"You're the prettiest girl here, Hannah. I want you to be my girlfriend." Ansel spoke smoothly, as if he had rehearsed this speech a hundred times. In fact, he had said it many times, each time using another girl's name.

"Ansel Bossé, I should tell your father and he will take a switch to your gluteus!" Ansel looked at Hannah and knitted his brows. He did not understand what a gluteus was, but he was all too familiar with a switch. "You should say your Hail Marys and go to confession!"

"Hannah, please don't tell my papa. I enjoy coming here and he'll make me stop if you tell him."

"Well, okay, but you need to do something for me."

"Sure, anything. What is it? You need something from the store?"

Hannah laughed. "You think I'm that kind of girl? No. I don't need you to sneak me any fancy ribbons or candy from the store. I want you to teach me how to drive your truck."

"Drive? Are you crazy? How am I going to do that? I only drive in the yard at our farm. What do you need to drive for, anyway? You have a bicycle; I've seen you ride it."

"I have an important job here helping the midwife Sister

Marie, and if I could learn to drive, she could go farther and help more people. The monks have a truck, but they can't always drive Sister Marie. If I could drive, maybe we could get another truck. You don't have to teach me now but you have to make me a promise that when I say it's time, you'll find a way to teach me."

"Well, I don't really see how that's going to work but sure, I'll teach you someday."

"I promise you Ansel, if you don't do it, you will suffer dearly."

"Got it. I'll do it."

"One more thing. Don't you ever kiss me again!"

"Sure, sure, I won't kiss you for sure."

The following year, two girls moved temporarily to the monastery from a neighboring village. Their mother had died in childbirth several years prior. Their father raised them through childhood and into their preteen years, but recently was fatally injured in a farming accident.

The girls, Arlette and La Roux Despins, were a year apart in age but inseparable, as if they had once occupied the womb together. They brushed each other's hair and picked out each other's clothes for the day. They sat together in the classroom and at meals and did their chores side by side. Despite repeated reprimands, the girls whispered and giggled frequently in the classroom. One day when the children arrived at the class-room, Sister Marguerite had rearranged the desks into clusters of four desks. The girls sat with their chair backs facing the center of the cluster and their desks projecting outward as if to create a pinwheel.

This new arrangement did not split the girls' symbiotic bond. They replaced the whispers with notes one would pass to the other or drop on her desk as she walked past. One night, long after lights out, Hannah caught the reflection of a candle flicker in the transom window of her room. She quietly slid out of bed and crept down the hallway until she spotted the burning candle in the library. Arlette and La Roux sat on the floor studying a human anatomy textbook. One would point, and the other would giggle. Hannah knew that if the Sisters caught them, they would suffer significant consequences. They would probably have three months' worth of extra chores and have to write essays and present them to the class.

Secretly, Hannah felt betrayed and a bit as if her elite status as a student of Sister Marie's had been violated. She was familiar with the book they were studying and, while not close enough to verify it, believed they were studying the male anatomy section of the text. Hannah had often studied the same images herself. Her work with Sister Marie allowed full access to the library. She studied the books on botanicals, husbandry, midwifery and anatomy freely in her spare time. She loved to read and learn and felt a special calling to understand the human body and how it worked.

The ink drawings of the male anatomy detailed the bulk and distinct muscle groups of the male physique. Some pictures showed the figure grossly contorted into unnatural postures to exaggerate various muscles. The head was drawn back severely with the chin to the side so the neck muscles could be demonstrated and labeled or the figure was leaning to one side then lifted from the waist and shifted into another dimension.

One image was particularly intriguing to Hannah. The male figure, penned in black ink on dusty cream paper, was seated, leaning back with his shoulders rounded forward and his head resting on his chest. His left arm was bent at the elbow with his hand resting on his right shoulder and his right arm wrapped around his waist. This fleshless figure was crumbled as if he had lost everything in the world and had no hope; yet every muscle in his body popped off the page like steel reinforcement from the world.

Most of the drawings showed the men with no genitalia. There was merely a horizontal line between the curvaceous thigh muscles. Hannah recalled being shocked the first time she saw the picture with the title "Male Human Anatomy". This was one of the few colored pictures in the book. The gluteus muscles were colored with dark red striations to match the lateral stomach muscles. Other muscles groups of the stomach and legs were pale pink. There were wisps of hair around what appeared to be two pouches suspended from the lower stomach muscles. Hannah had no point of reference, having never diapered a younger brother or seen a naked man.

She started observing the animals in the fields and noticed the differences between the genders. It was when she first saw one of the old plow horses in the field mounting another horse that she fully understood the act of procreation. For her, it was an act of nature. She had no notion of romance or lust and was somewhat perplexed by her classmates' giddiness as they studied the anatomical drawings.

Hannah drew in a breath and with the deepest sound she could muster cleared her throat. In an instant the girls blew out the candle, dropped the book and scampered to their room. Hannah snickered under her breath. The fright she gave them was lesson enough this time.

The girls did not learn their lesson, however. Not long after, La Roux was sneaking a peek at a crumpled note in her lap when Sister Marguerite walked up to La Roux's desk holding her hand out for the note. La Roux first crumpled the note into her fist and shook her head. Out came the blackboard pointer.

"Hand me that paper now, or you will have five cracks to your bottom at the front of the class. Heads down, the rest of you. Continue with your lessons."

La Roux hesitantly handed over the note. Sister Marguerite returned to her desk and opened it.

"La Roux Despins, who gave you this note?" La Roux hesitated again and refused to answer. "That's it young lady. You will have ten cracks and five Hail Marys."

"Sister Marguerite, it was me."

"Arlette Despins, you will also have five Hail Marys and you will read this note to the class."

"Sister Marguerite, I will do ten Hail Marys and a month of extra chores. Please, do not make me read the note." Arlette was nearly in tears, pleading her case. Hannah wondered what could be in that note to cause Arlette to volunteer for extra chores. The entire class knew she despised chores and frequently talked about her aunt and uncle coming to rescue them any day so they could get back to a 'normal' school.

"Unless you would also like ten cracks like your sister, you will come take this note and read it to the class. Now." Sister Marguerite was more upset than Hannah had ever seen her.

Arlette shuffled to Sister Marguerite's desk and slowly picked up the note. In a whispered, mumbling voice she read the note. "Next time you're alone with him in the cellar ask him to show you his."

The entire class gasped. Hannah felt queasy. She should have told on Ansel when he kissed her to protect the other girls. She stopped herself and rethought the note. Ansel or his brother, whoever "him" was in the note, is the one who needed protection!

A few weeks later, La Roux and Arlette left with their aunt and uncle. Ansel and his father continued to make deliveries. Noël did not return.

When the occasion arose, Ansel and Hannah talked about the parts of the truck and how they worked. Hannah was cautious about showing too much interest in driving while another Sister was present. Driving was left to the men. Hannah knew that she came to the convent under unusual circumstances and always tried to fly under the radar so as not to receive too much attention. She felt there was always a question about her commitment to the Order, given her exposure to Judaism as a young child. She never wanted to incite unwarranted concern.

Nearly a year later, a number of the Sisters planned a

weekend retreat at a neighboring parish. "The Sisters will be on retreat next week. Can you give me that driving lesson then?" Hannah knew Ansel was just as eager as she was to test the rules of the Sisters.

"I taught my mama to drive; I'm sure I can teach you. I will be here on Tuesday at noon." And so they planned their date.

With Tuesday morning's chores behind her, Hannah left the grounds for a walk down the country road. She told the remaining novitiates and students that she was going hunting for wild turnips. Ansel picked Hannah up about a kilometer from the monastery and took her to a pasture where the risks of accidental impact were minimal, or so they thought.

Hannah was much shorter than Ansel. The old truck was not equipped with an adjustable seat, so Hannah had to stretch her legs and body to reach the pedals. Once she got the truck in gear and released the clutch pedal, she could maneuver the vehicle perfectly. She practiced making turns and driving from one end of the pasture to the other.

Suddenly Ansel yelled, "Stop!"

Hannah looked over to Ansel to see what the problem was. They were in an empty field and there was no earthly purpose to stop right then.

"Cat. Stop!" Ansel pointed out to the barren field.

Hannah saw no cat, but panicked to think she might have run over the creature. In her panic, she confused the gas pedal with the clutch and propelled the truck into a dense thicket hedge bordering the field. The truck came to a sudden stop. Hannah flew out of the truck and followed the track behind the truck.

"What are you doing, Hannah? Did you hit your head? Are you okay?"

"Help me. We have to find the cat. It might be injured."

Ansel roared with laughter. Hannah stared at him.

"It's you who has hit your head. What can you be laughing at? Come, help me look for the cat."

"There is no cat. It's a trick to test your reflexes. That's how my papa taught me to be quick with my feet and to pay attention to the road."

Hannah ran to him and hit his arm with her fist. "How dare you do that to me? Oh, no! Look at your truck with its nose in the weeds. I hope we can get it to run. It's a long way back to the monastery if I have to walk."

"Ah, that old thing is made for a little beating. It's fine. Get in. I'll drive you home." Ansel backed the truck out of the thicket. They inspected the front end and noted some fresh scratches, but no serious damage. "Gives her character."

While they were stopped Ansel showed Hannah where to add gas and oil and how to jiggle the spark plug wires for better connectivity after hard rains.

The following week, when Ansel made a delivery to the convent, Sister Agnes commented on the condition of the truck. "Ansel, your old truck is looking a bit worse for wear. I hope you are saving up for a replacement."

"Oh yes, Sister, I am saving up. Really though, her cosmetics may be rough and she may have tried to smell some roses recently but her engine is strong." Ansel glanced at Hannah, who quickly turned her back to avoid notice of the silent giggles.

Hannah felt at ease in Ansel's company. Over the years she used him as a sounding board for many things. He appeared without his father mid-week at times to make an extra delivery. After a few years, he made all the deliveries without his father. Some days he had the leisure of lingering at the monastery and Hannah would take him into the garden or out to the fields to look at the livestock. They consulted with one another on a variety of issues. Hannah was the first to know he had a serious girlfriend and when the time came, that he was planning to marry her. Theirs was a long and lasting, loving friendship.

15

SOLACE FOR SALLY

"Sally, you are the most beautiful of God's creations I have ever witnessed." George traced the silhouette of Sally's delicate face against the late afternoon sun, trailing off to lose his fingers in her dark, soft curls. They were both exhausted yet giddy and bursting with passion as they sat on the bed.

Sally looked out onto the water of the bay as the warm and brilliant blue of the day faded, melding into the dark sky as the sun set. A nightly mating ritual of the night and the water: the water and air become one and lie together, waking in the morning in splendid glory to serve the earth. Sally was envious of the peace and ease of the elements.

Mindlessly her fingers caressed his inner thigh as her thoughts turned to a time long ago on a beach far away. She recalled excitement as the family piled out of their car at Standbad Wannsee. She was about five years old and had not seen the beach before. There were people everywhere. Sally did not own a bathing suit and giggled to see the pale men in their underwear running into the water. Women in dresses with babies at their breasts took shelter under little huts. Children played in the sand, taking turns burying each other. Sally's mother had learned to swim here when she was a young girl, before the signs were posted prohibiting those of Jewish faith on the beach.

To Sally the water felt fresh, although it looked like mud. With her parents' permission she kicked off her shoes, hiked up her dress and ran joyously into the water. At first she waded cautiously. The water crept up her legs, past her calves, then her knees, and finally to the bottom of her thighs.

"Sarah, come on back here," Mama called. Reluctantly, Sally returned to stand before her. "Here, let's take your dress off. You can swim in your underclothes."

Sally had protested when Mama told her to wear an undershirt that morning. "It's too hot Mama!"

"Trust me Sarah, you will want it when you get to the place we are going today."

She obeyed her mother, still curious where the family was going but not daring to ask again. She had stopped asking when Papa warned her that if she asked one more time, they would not be going.

Sally took her dress off and ran back to the water in undershirt and panties, not the least bit intimidated by her attire or the water. She spent the afternoon imitating the teens that could swim. She sat underwater and practiced holding her breath as long as she could. Papa played with her. He threw her, and she sailed through the air, landing with a splash and a giggle. Mama swam farther off shore, alone. Isaac complained that the water was too cold. He only went into the water to fill a pail, then return to the sand to build sand sculptures with other children on the beach.

Sally loved being at the beach that day. Their family was one of the last to leave. In the car on the way home, Isaac shivered beside her in the backseat. She had stripped off her wet undergarments and was warm and happy in the dry dress and sweater that Mama had thoughtfully packed.

"Papa that was amazing! I love the beach. I want to go there every day."

"Did you see your mother swim, Sarah? Like a fish in the ocean, isn't she?"

"I'm a good swimmer too, Papa. Did you see me swim, Mama?"

"Yes, Sarah, I did, and I am very proud of you. You were a good swimmer today. Maybe we will get to swim again another day and I will teach you more strokes."

"What's a stroke, Mama?"

"They are the ways to move your hands and your legs to make you go really fast in the water."

"Well, I think you kids will sleep very well tonight. Isaac, did you have fun?" There was no response. Isaac had fallen fast asleep, exhausted from the long day playing in the sun.

"Where are you?" George pulled Sally closer to him and wrapped her securely in his arms. The beat of his heart pulsated into her cheek as it rested heavily on his chest. This faraway look on her face was familiar. He sensed a secret world lived in her head. He never pushed her to talk about what seemed to be a dark place lying deep within. After all, she was present enough with him to have a good time. They even talked about a future together.

Sally gave in to his embrace, allowing her passion to come to life. They made love, again. George, strong and fit yet gentle and kind, was the perfect compliment to Sally's timid, cautious, yet playful nature. He brought out the best in her, here in the cabin on the lake and back at school.

Both were spent from simultaneous orgasms that roared through their core, consuming the last of their energy like a raging fire. Their skin stuck together with droplets of sweat from the latest play. They lay talking before moving to the kitchen for the last meal together before heading back to college. This time together was rare and precious. Their studies were demanding, and privacy was elusive.

Thanks to their friend John, they were able to enjoy this time together, away from studies and unwanted intrusions. John invited them to use his family's cabin on Buzzards Bay just outside New Bedford. John and his family were traveling abroad for the Easter holiday. Sally and George had visited the cabin with John and his family months prior and fell in love with the area. Both were renewed after spending time on the water and hiking through the woods. The nearby small communities were relaxed and welcoming.

"Sal, I've decided not to graduate this year. I'm going to stay on and get my architect's credentials. I will graduate next year." George knew he was opening himself up for Sally's intimacy dance, but he couldn't keep it from her any longer. The school year would soon end, and she expected him to leave then for Chicago.

Sally couldn't look at George. She had to be certain this was his decision and his alone. She had avoided thinking about his leaving this weekend. It frightened her.

"Sal, did you hear me? Say something."

"Of course I heard you. You have that offer in Chicago—a terrific offer with a top engineering firm. Why would you give that up?"

"I can think of a lot of reasons Sal, and I know you don't want to hear them all." Any mention of maintaining a long-distance relationship soured their talks about his job offer. She had said more than once, with no rational basis, that it would not work.

Finally, Sally turned to him. Her dark eyes locked with his beautiful blue eyes, looking to her for approval. "George, I can't be your reason. You have so much opportunity before you now; I will not stand in your way. I know what it's like to have a dream and then watch it crumble before it comes to life. I don't want that to happen to you."

With that Sally bit her lip, something George had watched her do a thousand times in the three years he'd known her. She

79

had more to say and someday she would, but for now he just wanted to love her in all her delicate beauty.

George and Sally met during her first year of teacher's college at Providence City College. George was a sophomore studying civil engineering at Brown University. He and his friend John were helping John's cousin Doris move into a rooming house. Doris, like Sally, was a new student at City College and they were living in the same rooming house.

Sally's uncle and mother drove her from their home in New York on that same day. Unlike Doris, Sally did not need help with moving in; her belongings fit into two suitcases. Uncle Morris carried these to her room while she said goodbye to her mother on the front lawn.

Sally and her mother were very close. Together they had lived a life never fully revealed to anyone. When they first stood on the soil of the United States, they made a pact that they would never look back, only ahead. Sally was too young then to know the turmoil that this pact would create within her soul and psyche. Nonetheless, to this point they fulfilled that pact, and Sally had no intention of breaking the silence. Uncle Morris had some knowledge of their life before but never pried, as he too had similar unspeakable experiences.

"Sally, if your father could be here today you have to know just how very proud he would be. You have been an exceptional daughter, and you will be a superior teacher. I am so honored that God chose me to be your mother." Sally's mother wiped a tear from the corner of her eye.

"Oh, Mama, you are the best! I miss you and Uncle Morris already."

Morris gave her a hearty hug. "You mind your studies young lady and ignore those boys. You remember what I told you. They are nothing but trouble."

"Oh course. But if I meet any like you, I may have to rethink your advice. You couldn't cause trouble if you wanted to."

Morris had been her rock while girlfriends had their fathers to lean on. He helped her with her studies in high school, her college application, and stood in like a father as a chaperone at school dances. She loved her mother but sometimes only a man could provide an answer. Even today as they drove to Providence, she queried him about politics and literature, two subject her mother declined to opine about. Yes, she would miss them both.

Sally waved to Mother and Uncle Morris. As she turned to walk up the front steps of the wrap-around porch of the boarding house, she heard a car rush up the street and come to a sudden screeching stop in front of the house. At the sound of the squealing tires, Sally turned toward the commotion. It was a red 1950 Studebaker Commander convertible, a fact she knew only from conversations with Uncle Morris.

A huge storage locker jutted up from the backseat and jolted toward the driver's head, just missing it before settling against the backrest of the rear seat. Beside the locker sat a beautiful woman with a huge smile framed by ruby red lips. The young man sitting in the front passenger's seat hopped out of the car. The woman grabbed his hand, stood up on the seat and hopped out over the door.

Sally looked past the boy to the young woman. She was wearing the trendiest of black and white pencil-leg pedal pushers and a bright coral fitted top that showed off an exquisite body. Big white glasses with dark as night lenses shielded her eyes and a white silk scarf elegantly draped her head with blonde waves peeking out along her face. Polished toenails peeked out from strappy gold sandals.

Sally's fashion sense was nil. She went to a public school in a neighborhood that housed immigrants with modest incomes like their own. Her clothes were austere, either made by her mother or bought at the local department store. She shunned fashion magazines and never set foot inside a boutique. "They are for the pompous and shamelessly wealthy," she recalled telling a friend as they passed a newsstand on a rare unescorted trip to the movies.

"Hey doll, can you give me a hand?" The Vogue-looking model extended a hatbox in Sally's direction.

"Uh, sure." Sally reached for the string suspending the box. "I'm Sally. Happy to lend a hand but are you sure you're at the right place?"

"Doris, doll, and yeah, this is the right address. Not my idea. Daddy thought it would be good for me to live with the ordinary. I don't mean any offense by that, but my dreams are much bigger than living on Oak Street in a rooming house."

"No offense taken, I don't think." Sally wasn't sure what to make of Doris. The women on the cover of Vogue never talked back to her, so she wasn't quite sure what to expect out of someone who looked like them.

"Daddy says that my ideas about bettering the world by teaching about cognitive dissonance and behavioral conditioning are pie in the sky ideas and I need to get a little grounding. In reality, I think he is trying to get me to drop out and get married so I can enjoy the fruit of my husband's labors rather than forge my own way."

"Cognitive what?" Sally thought to herself. *"Behavioral conditioning? Maybe those Vogue models have tutors or something. Just another way to show off."*

"Doris here thinks men are conditioned for only two things, food and, well, that other thing, and she feels it's her womanly duty to teach girls that they can condition them to do housework too." The young man held out his hand. "I'm John, by the way, and this is my buddy George."

Sally stood there in a simple, boring dress, tied at the waist with her special black ribbon. She wore sturdy, utilitarian saddle shoes. Suddenly the comfort of the modest homes and working-class neighborhood slipped from under her. She was on edge, feeling out of place by the apparent sophistication of these new arrivals.

She held her hand out to each in turn. "Pleasure to meet you John, George. By the way, I think you are brilliant, Doris. I concur and have found Debbie's Cakes to be the best edible reward for conditioning."

Sally had done no such thing. She had no idea where that lie came from. Maybe something Uncle Morris had said? It didn't matter. Based on the reaction of her new acquaintances, what she said was not that stupid. The young men rolled their eyes and laughed as they reached for the trunk from the back seat of the car.

Sally grabbed Doris's other hatboxes and together they flew up the front porch steps. The mistress of the house stood on the landing, holding the screen door open for them.

"Hello Aunt Tilly," Doris greeted the lady of the house.

"Doris, dear, it's so good to see you. I see you are still filled with fire and spirit! Your father didn't say you had a beau. Who are these good-looking lads with you?"

"Matilda Brown, this is my mother's brother's son John James and his friend George Hunt. John rows for Brown University and occasionally studies journalism. George is a brilliant scholar at Brown studying engineering. He is here from Detroit, Michigan."

"Pleasure to meet you all. Come in. Put those things in Doris's room, third door on the left just up those stairs, then come back down and join me in the kitchen for some lemonade and cookies."

The boys bounded up the stairs to deliver Doris's trunk. As Aunt Tilly headed down the hallway, Sally turned to Doris with a quizzical look. "Aunt Tilly is my father's sister. She married for love and was cut out of Grandpa's will. She swears it was the right decision. Uncle Frank passed a couple of years ago, but they had an extraordinarily happy life. She says being rich has nothing to do with what you have in the bank or how many cars or homes you have; it is all about being surrounded by those you love and who love you, finding happiness in every day and retiring at night knowing you have made life better for someone that day."

Sally was not yet aware, but a whole new level of education was unfolding. There were lessons beyond books and classes awaiting her. Lessons of the heart had begun.

"Sally, honey, what is it?" They were packing up to return to the life of school and grown-up decisions. Sally was lost in thought about her parents. There were times when she missed her father immensely. This was one of them, although she wasn't sure she missed him or missed whom she dreamt he would be if he were still living. Her heart was raw and aching with memories. Will George disappear the way her father did?

Sally shifted her focus to the present and to George. "George, I…"

She stopped and tried to quiet her mind before continuing. She felt as if her lie of a life would come flooding out if she opened her mouth again. Swallowing hard, she turned and headed back to the cabin for another armful of things to pack into the car. On her return, she finally faced George. "I know you will do what you feel is right for you. The architecture certificate seems very important to you."

George moved closer to Sally and took her hands. "Sal, someday I will build you a beautiful home where your grand-children can play, you can paint or do whatever, and we can lie together in our huge bed and remember this day."

With that, George dropped to one knee in the dirt behind the car between the ocean and the cabin. "Sally Fischer, will you marry me?"

Sally tugged on George to get him up off the ground, buried her head in his chest and whispered, "Yes George Hunt, I will marry you."

Tears streamed down her face, seeping into the place where her face met his chest. Filled with relief, he let the tears soak in, a reminder of how close they had become and of the well, hidden deep within this wonderful woman whose secrets he may never know.

George gently lifted her chin, bringing her eyes to meet his. He gently massaged the wetness on her cheeks. "I will love you to the end of time Sal, that I promise you."

16

GERTIE BIDS BERLIN FAREWELL

"Mama, take that awful rag off your head!"

Gertie hated the once-bright pink silk scarf that her mother wore every spring season, now faded with nearly a decade of wear. Gertie and her mother had received matching scarves from Gertie's father years before. She remembered a day when she was about eight. The family was walking to the May Day parade. Mama's scarf was flapping in the wind and Gertie's scarf was cinched around her waist. Once fashionable, it was now dated and clashed with Mama's tinted blue-black hair, bright red lips and rouge painted cheeks. She wore the scarf draped over her head and tied under her chin. She looked old and dated. Everything about her mother embarrassed Gertie these days. If she actually cared more, she would hate her mother.

As the time neared for her to leave for college, Gertie grew increasingly curious and confused about what had happened to the Jewish friends she had in childhood. One rare night at home with her mother and stepfather, she inquired of those childhood friends. "Do you remember my friends Sarah and Hannah?"

"Sure I do Gertie. Sarah and her mom went to that garden

tea party with us. They lived in that house the Bergs live in now just down the street. You know, I have a picture from the newspaper taken when you were a little girl at the Maypole dance. I think your friends might be in that picture as well."

Gertie's mother brought a box of papers out of the closet and rummaged through them. From the middle of the box she pulled out a newspaper. There on the front page was a picture of children smiling at the camera with a Maypole standing tall behind them, loose streamers hanging from the pole waving in the breeze. "Here you are." Gertie's mother pointed to a younger Gertie, hair pulled back into a braid and a wide toothy grin.

"Here is Sarah." Gertie pointed to a girl standing off to the side of her. "And that is her brother. I don't remember his name now."

Gertie studied the picture, pointed out a couple other children she knew, and then spotted Hannah slightly deeper in the crowd. "Here is Hannah." She held her finger just below Hannah's face as she extended the paper to Mother.

"Oh yes, her papa worked at the bank. Her mama was a seamstress. She did some sewing for me."

"Mama, where did they go? They never came back to school after May Day, and we never got to play again. Papa said they moved away, but they never said goodbye."

"May Day, did you say? Which one?" Gertie's stepfather inquired.

"It was about 1938 I think."

"That sounds about right. For one of the exercises our troops had to gather up the Jews to work in the factories and work camps. Maybe they got caught up in that and were relocated for the war effort. I was deployed up north, but I heard that's how they got workers sometimes. I would think they would have been released and come back home by now, though." Gertie's stepfather spoke in an annoying, emotionless monotone.

"What do you mean they gathered them up? Mama, do you know what he's talking about?"

"I remember on that day your father invited all the neighbors to come to the Maypole dance. We left the park before it was over because he wasn't feeling well. I don't know anything about anybody going to work camps. I did think it odd they just disappeared without saying goodbye, but we left shortly after that ourselves for a trip to Oma's and by the time we came home I guess I was distracted." Gertie knew Mama was not that observant and had become very involved again in her church activities. Nonetheless, something just did not feel right.

That night Gertie lay in bed and tried to remember the day in the park when she last saw her friends. Panic gripped her as she thought about what she had learned about the fate of many Jews and the disappearance of her friends. They were her friends. They played the same games, shared toys, chased butterflies and picked flowers together, sat in class and ate lunch together. They could have been her sisters. She refused to believe they had been taken away but could not reconcile why they had not said goodbye.

Over the next several weeks, while marking time until she could get away to University, Gertie made inquiries in the neighborhood about her friends but did not learn anything. She tried to find teachers from their grammar school but could locate none. Few people in the neighborhood were there in those earlier years.

Gertie became more flexible with her appearance and even occasionally dated. She loved to swing dance and party. She had acquaintances throughout the city and was no stranger to foreign soldiers. She was not easily intimidated and, perhaps due to early travel experiences, was not shy about introducing herself to strangers. She was a runner for the black market, shuttling cigarettes, candy and liquor. She continued to do well in school, but the teachers worried about her political posturing. She wrote school papers that were anti-government and they suspected she was involved in anti-government leagues.

One teacher encouraged Gertie to go on to University. He recognized the quality of Gertie's writing, although the subject matter was provocative. He forwarded one of her essays to a University in London that was admitting women. The result was an invitation for Gertie to apply and eventually be accepted to that University. Little did the teacher know that Gertie already had guaranteed access to University; but it pleased her to know that she had the academic ability to attain admission in her own right.

At seventeen Gertie was heading for London to study. She looked forward to starting life in a new place. Black market money and some inheritance would buy time before she had to get a job. Her mother and stepfather sold the family home and would retire to the country. A portion of the proceeds would be given to Gertie to pay tuition. Gertie did not tell them that free tuition had already been secured by Sabine.

As she walked up the stairs to the airplane, she turned back one last time to wave to her mother, standing below with the ugly old pink silk scarf flapping in the wind.

17

ENLIGHTENMENT

Hannah retched for days. Her stomach was long-since emptied of anything that may have poisoned her generally impenetrable vitality. Sister Marie administered several herbal teas that Hannah knew to be first-line treatments for stomach ailments. Some concoctions she tried were new combinations of remedies, but Hannah was in no state to care about the qualities or interactions of the herbs. Her body was failing her. It was as if it was starving her for no good reason.

"Hannah, our bodies house more than our hearts and our intestines. They are the vessel in which we store our soul and our memories, our faith and our fears. You have purged your body and still have not rid yourself of whatever it is that needs to be expelled. I have prayed for guidance. I believe I understand that what is going on right now is not illness with your body. There is some dis-ease with your soul. Do you understand what I am saying?"

"I understand your words, Sister Marie, but I do not know what underlies this exhausting retching. I will pray for guidance as well and open myself to God's answers."

Hannah missed the garden and her work with Sister Marie.

She hoped to find answers so she could return to her studies and work. That evening, after silently praying, she lay listening to the long arms of the willows scratch the roof of the sleeping quarters in the breeze. As she drifted off to sleep, Hannah saw her family as she remembered them in Berlin, just as if it was present day. She saw her friends and her neighborhood. Joy filled the air in those early days. Suddenly, there were images of soldiers, darkness and cramped spaces, the sound of a gunshot and whimpering.

Hannah's hands inched along the cold stones of a dark corridor. She heard water dripping in the distance and muffled voices. Slowly she moved toward a light, filled with panic.

As she neared the light, she found herself huddled against the wall of a cave facing two large underground rooms. The room on the left was faintly lit by a distant fire throwing shadows across the room. Three figures stood deep in the darkness, lit by the occasional flicker leaning in their direction. Two of the shadows were familiar, the third was not.

To the right was a room filled with sunlight beaming in from a natural skylight in the rocks. There was music in this room. Again, there were three figures in the room. They were animated. Their faces were peaceful, and they wore smiles. She recognized two of them as her parents. She looked back to the darkened room and inched closer to get a better look. The room was daunting. She found herself cowering. A revolting stench came from the room. She was overtaken by fear and awakened to the muffled sounds of her own scream and sobs.

Sister Marie placed her hands on Hannah's forehead and forearm. "Hannah, its Sister Marie. You are safe. You are fine."

She repeated this over and over, like a mantra, until Hannah was willing to open her eyes. She knew that either she would still be in that scary dark place or she would have to talk about it. After the screaming stopped she lay in silence, seeking comfort and understanding from the horrific feelings she awoke with. Finally, she opened her eyes and looked into Sister Marie's eyes. "Where are my parents?"

Sister Marie was taken aback by the question and reached to feel Hannah's cheeks for fever. The Sisters had never hidden the reality of Hannah's arrival at the monastery from her. Now, at fifteen, she was well aware of the story of whence she came. "Hannah, you know your parents passed away on your journey here."

"Where do their souls reside, Sister? Are they in hell or do they rest with God in heaven?" Tears streamed down her face and she clenched her rosary tight. "I just cannot bear to believe that because they were Jewish they do not get to bask in the glory of our Heavenly Father."

"Oh dear child, our God is a merciful God, and he welcomes all who seek His kingdom to reside with him there. I feel strongly that your parents are with our good Lord, smiling down on you as they see the incredible woman and healer you have become. God is good Hannah and, while some of our teachings portray Him as harsh, I walk in his light every day knowing that His goodness overcomes all the evils in the world. Rest easily, Sister. Your parents lost their lives saving yours, much as Jesus did. Who more than they are deserving of salvation?"

Calmness overcame Hannah. She drifted off to a dreamless sleep. When she awoke, it felt as if a tremendous weight had been lifted and her spirits were bright. Her appetite returned, and she returned to her studies and work with Sister Marie with a renewed sense of hope for the patients she saw thereafter.

PART III

BEYOND BERLIN – ADULTHOOD

18

SALLY, WOMAN EVOLVING

"Roger Frankel."
"Margaret Gooding."
Rona Fischer took a deep breath as tears welled in her eyes. The City College president would call her daughter next. Her heart swelled with pride and gratitude.

"Sally Fischer."

Sally walked across the stage draped in a black commencement gown. Around her neck were the golden tassels of a degree with honors. She was always a good student and didn't fail her mother in college. She walked cautiously in new high heels, a gift from her friend Doris. As she approached the President, a smile unfolded across her face.

With an equally brilliant smile, George leaned in his future mother-in-law's direction and whispered to Rona, "Soon to be Sally Hunt."

"Don't forget, it was Sally Fischer who walked across that stage, George. We can't forget what she has accomplished on her own." George was very proud of her. The past year they had both focused intently on their studies. They saw one another weekly and on rare occasions slipped out of town for a weekend together. They each spent winter break with their own family, and spring break completing final school projects. George finished his architecture certification the prior month and interviewed for several jobs.

Not much time was spent on another celebration they were having in just a few weeks. With school finished for both of them, they planned to be married before the big move to Chicago. Sally's mother had taken two weeks off from work to help Sally prepare for the wedding. They planned for it to be small and simple.

Doris, however, had other thoughts. She, too, was graduating from City College. She had settled into life in the boarding house and earned her degree in sociology. She wrote several articles during her school career, which were well received by the psychology and sociology communities. Several offers to join graduate programs came her way, but she elected to stay in the area to earn an advanced degree in literature. Sally suspected that her love interest, a local businessman, had something to do with that choice.

On graduation day Uncle Morris took them out for lunch. Doris's family joined them later at Tilly's house to continue the celebration. The women gathered in the kitchen to make wedding plans while the men sat in the yard sharing a cigar and drinking cold beer. Sally was going to miss Tilly. She has become a wonderful stand-in for her own mother and was much easier to talk to in some regards. A great confidante, Tilly knew when to keep a secret and when to share her own. She was an open book, which made it safe to share with her. Sally never talked about her past but found comfort in being able to talk about what married life would be like and how to balance career and family.

Mrs. Michaud, Doris's mother, joined in with the planning and by the end of the night all the essential decisions were made and a plan of attack was in place. The cake was sketched out and Mrs. Michaud was going to see the baker the following day. It would be two tiers with satin smooth white icing and two silver wedding bells on top. They would place yellow and purple flowers on the altar. The bride would carry a bouquet of bright pink roses with yellow and purple flowers mixed in to tie everything together.

Tilly had already started Sally's dress. Her mother wanted to make it, but agreed months prior that it was more practical for Tilly to make it since long-distance fittings were impossible. Tilly took the women to her sewing room to show them the progress. When Tilly opened the door, they all fell silent. The seamstress' form in the middle of the room wore a snow-white silk dress in a simple design that would show off Sally's tiny waist and fall just below the knees. The neckline was low enough to frame Sally's delicate collarbones and dressed with a shiny satin collar for a very sophisticated look. The lace sleeves were fitting for a church wedding but could be removed for a less formal affair. Tilly had finished the armholes and showed Sally how she could easily take the stitching out to take off the sleeves later. Sally had insisted on a dress that she could wear in the future and not store in a box. It may be a bit too fancy to wear to work, but she imagined wearing it to George's office Christmas party, if they had one.

"I have the perfect earrings, dear, for something borrowed," Mrs. Michaud offered. Each of the women in turn offered something old, new and blue to complete the ensemble. Sally and her mother planned to go shopping the following day for shoes, which would satisfy the new.

Doris was the maid of honor. During Christmas break she shopped and found the dress she thought would be perfect for the wedding. "Sally, you have got to see what I got for your wedding."

Sally thought maybe she had found decorations for the church. Holding Sally's hand, Doris led her into the room. There, lying on the bed, was a bright pink pile of tulle.

"What is this?" Sally had never seen so much fabric in one dress.

"Wait, wait! Go back to your room and I'll try it on for you. You just have to see it on." Doris pushed her out of the room and changed into the dress.

"Now what do you say."

When Doris walked back into Sally's room, she looked as if she was walking down a Paris runway. The dress fit like a glove around bosom and waist. Tulle overtook the satin for the skirt that landed at the knees. Her shoulders were bare. She had pulled her hair up and put on lipstick and high heels.

"Stunning. You will take all the focus off the bride, and frankly, I am fine with that. I would rather just elope but it's important to my mother that we have a ceremony." She could not imagine picking such a fancy bridesmaid's dress for a simple wedding, but she would not tell Doris. The dress was beautiful and very flattering on Doris, who was not one for subtlety.

By the big day, everything was ready. George's parents arrived the day before the wedding. Sally's belongings were packed and ready at Tilly's house. She and her mother had a good time talking about setting up house and making lists of things to do and get when they moved into their house in Chicago.

The wedding was in a Lutheran church not far from Tilly's. Sally went to this church frequently, and George joined her on occasion. She felt at home there, as much as any place. George was raised as a Methodist, but his priorities during school did not include much time in worship. Together George and Sally attended holiday services. They each felt as if some sense of ritual would enrich their life together. They shared the desire to introduce their future children to some traditions that were influential in their own childhoods. Christmas evening candlelight services, Easter sunrise services and Maundy Thursday were some of the most impactful services they shared.

They chose a Saturday morning to be married. The honeymoon would be the road trip to Chicago, and they wanted to be on the road as early as possible.

Sally wanted the focus to be on the marriage, not the pomp and circumstance. Her wedding visions did not include a live band and late night dancing, drunkenness and debauchery. This was a sacred event for her. She would have been happy to have only the audience of the minister with the emphasis being on the vows, but she knew it was important to her mother that there be a celebration of sorts.

Sally cherished the simplicity of her dress and the fact that it was specially made for her with the hands of her beloved surrogate mother Tilly. Doris's flamboyant dress brought her personality to life, and Sally was not the least bit threatened that it would take away from the moment. Everyone on their invitation list knew Doris and her love of fashion and fun.

Sally was so grateful that her mother took the time to come help her with the preparations. She had a diplomatic way of negotiating the decorations. Her help in toning down the cake to something less gaudy and more in keeping with Sally's tastes was much appreciated. Sally felt as if she would get married every year if she and her mother could be this close and have as much fun. They had silently suffered so much over the years; the loss of identity, loss of family and home, and dissolution from their faith. Sally would forever be grateful for her mother's love and commitment. There was not a moment that she felt she had taken her for granted.

It was a beautiful day. The intimacy of the ceremony, with only two dozen of their friends and family in attendance, made it extra-special for Sally and George. The meaning of their union did not get lost in the chaos of a large group. They socialized with and exchanged hugs with all in attendance. Uncle Morris, handsome in his dark suit, walked Sally down the aisle. Once again she missed her father, but was grateful for Morris's role in her life. The couple exchanged simple gold bands, and a church soloist provided the music. In less than thirty minutes the ceremony was over. Sally's mother insisted on hiring a photographer to capture the day. "Especially," she mourned, "because you will be so far away in Chicago and I don't know when I will see you again."

The photographer took pictures of the wedding party and the attendees since it was such a small group, and then excused most while he photographed only the bride, groom and parents.

The wedding reception was right there in the church basement. They served only cake, coffee and champagne. There were no gifts, but the couple received several envelopes with cash to help them reach their destination. With no music and dancing, the reception wound down in about an hour and it was soon time for the happy couple to leave. Sally made the rounds, hugging all the women. She unclipped Mrs. Michaud's earrings and handed them to her. Mrs. Michaud closed Sally's hand around the jewelry and told her to keep them. "These are so beautiful on you and I have plenty of jewelry. Please keep them. If for any reason you find yourself in dire straits for cash, you can sell these. But I have a feeling your handsome husband there will take great care of you."

"Oh, Mrs. Michaud, thank you so very much, for these and for everything. Do come visit us in Chicago." Sally threw her arms around Doris's mother and hugged her before moving on to her dear friend Doris.

"Ya know doll, I didn't know what to make of you that first day we met but I knew one thing for certain. You were good and truly good people are hard to come by. I'm going to miss you bushels, but am so happy for you. And you know you have to come back next spring for my wedding, right?" Doris and Sally embraced for a long time before Sally pulled away.

"I'll write. Study hard now and finish school. I can't wait to see what you do after that!" Sally gave Doris a final peck on the cheek and whispered "I love you like a sister" into her ear. Doris grabbed a hanky and dabbed her eyes. She felt the same.

Sally and George reached Chicago, set up house and started new jobs. George worked for an engineering and architectural firm. Sally taught high school English, a position she was passionate about. They settled into a rental home in the suburbs of north Chicago. George's promise to build a home rested on their mind's shelf of hopes and dreams, waiting for the right time. The first year went smoothly. They did not return for Doris's wedding. She and her beau eloped during the winter when they discovered that she was pregnant and she dropped out of school.

It was not until the end of the second year in Chicago that they managed to get a vacation. George had a week off and Sally was on summer break from teaching.

"Where did you go?" The words disappeared into the darkness, fusing with the glassy facade of the lake. Shadows of clouds and trees fell onto the water. Her belly absorbed the last heat of the day from the weathered planks of the dock. The eyes of a much younger self looked back at her from the water's surface, pleading to be brought to life.

"Are you talking to the fish again? I told you, the more noise you make the harder they are to catch."

George tapped at her feet with his own as he stood over her. "How about you just go in there and talk to them directly?"

He reached over and cradled her tiny waist in his broad hands, lifting as if to heave her head first in to the lake. Sally found her footing as he suspended her over the dock. She turned to find his eyes, laying to rest again the shadow of the girl she once was, with a story she was too terrified to share.

"So that's the way you want to play this, huh? Who's making the noise now?" She threw her arms around his neck and pulled him close, pressing her lips against his to silence them. George lifted his lips from hers. His cheek glided against hers until his lips reached her ear. "Let's go back to my place."

He picked her up and carried her to the tent. Like wild

animals rutting in spring with their bodies rooted into the earth, they ambitiously and with wild abandon made love. There may have been a howl or two from that tent, reaching out to the heavens with no one but the animals to bear witness. Sally lost herself during sex with George. Barriers to inhibition, self-scrutiny and fear of secrets ceased to exist. If time and physical stamina allowed, she would nurture these moments, so they grew to become time itself, with moments of real life interspersed.

They fell asleep late in the night with stars dancing over-head and the subtle sound of water lapping against the shore. Sally awoke to the smell of slowly burning pine on the camp-fire and cooking flesh in the frying pan. George had gotten up early and caught breakfast. He prepped the cast iron camp skillet with lard before putting the trout in to fry.

Sally felt it. It was a new day, a fresh start. The birds chased one another from branch to branch. Some jays investigated the campsite, looking for discarded food. A canoe glided across the lake. Sally panicked for a moment, fearing they had overlooked another camper in the area during their lovemaking escapade the night before. She looked around to discover a jeep parked near the dock that surely was not there the prior evening.

"Don't worry; they pulled in about an hour ago." George had a keen sense of her thoughts.

"Who says I was worrying? I'm an exhibitionist at heart."

Later, Sally pegged this as when their firstborn, Janna, was conceived. Janna loved the outdoors and was happiest in the water. It soothed her in a way Sally never could. She was an easy baby, all things considered, but as with all children, she had her moments. At those times, Sally drew a bath and let Janna play in the water. Immediately she calmed. She swam at an early age and as a grown woman with children of her own, Janna swam, boated, and fished regularly.

19

INTRODUCING SISTER ANNA

Hannah stood just inside the kitchen and took in the scene unfolding there. The kitchen vibrated with excitement as each Sister managed her station. Humming and soft singing could be heard when pots weren't clanging, and cleavers were still. Sister Aguilar's head was enveloped in garlicky steam rising from a roaster just pulled from the oven. A huge leg of lamb rested beneath the cover of the roaster with juices oozing from the meat and dripping into the bottom of the pan. She lifted the lid and sampled the juices then poked the meat to measure its doneness. After dousing it with more salt, she covered it again and placed it back in the oven, before moving on to test the next one. In all, Hannah counted six large pans in the massive dark metal ovens. Never before had she seen all the ovens in operation.

Sister Albertine stood to the right of the stove preparing pies on the wooden counter. She slammed the wooden rolling pin onto the counter with such force Hannah thought it would break. Like a gifted professional baker, she smoothed the pie dough into the pie tin and filled it with great proficiency before topping with a layer of dough sprinkled with cinnamon and sugar. One dozen apple pies were quickly assembled. She turned next to a copper bowl filled with lemons that would soon be juiced and transformed into lemon cake.

In the center of the kitchen stood a long wooden work-table. Root vegetables gathered from the cellar were being prepared. A large trash bin was being filled with shavings and clippings. The three nuns at this station created a rhythm as they prepared the vegetables. The Sister wielding a large cleaver chopped off the unusable root and stem with a definitive 'thud' against the cutting board. The vegetable was passed to the next Sister in line to be peeled with "swishes" that went so fast they became one long continuous sound. The vegetables were then rinsed and diced or sliced. Using a much smaller knife Sister Grace stealthily and precisely created the prescribed size vegetable for the soup, stew, the roasted vegetable and goose cassoulet being assembled.

Plum and lemon tarts and jars of preserves lined the serving buffet. Bread dough filled several large bowls, rising in the warmth of the room until it was time to bake croissants and dinner rolls. Lemons and basil, freshly washed in the sink, would be used to create soufflés just before dinner was ready to be served.

"Sister Anna Maria," Sister Margaret called out.

Hannah's mind was lost in the bustle of the nuns in the kitchen and the friars carrying linens, crystal, and serving dishes to the large dining room. She barely heard Sister Margaret, the choir's lone baritone, through her thoughts and the distractions throughout the monastery.

Hannah was comfortable at the monastery with no desire to explore beyond the confines of the community. She wanted to continue to study with the Sisters who had adopted her as part of their family. Making the decision to join the order at age sixteen was easy for her. At that time she donned the tradi-tional clay-gray garb of a Novice. Initially, the white starched veil irritated her delicate skin, but she adjusted and soon wore it like a second hide. Through the process of adopting this new family and committing to God for life, she left behind the young Hannah Amalie with the fractured childhood and weeping heart, and came to be known as Sister Anna Maria. She felt as if a new life and opportunity to start afresh had been breathed into her.

"Sister Anna Maria. Go out to the garden and gather flowers to decorate the tables."

Anna nodded and turned to the magnificent blooming garden, framed like a watercolor painting in the large windows of the dining hall. She stepped through the doorway onto a cobblestone path with herbs bountiful on either side. The scent of thyme mingled with the perfume of lavender, its cheerful purple flowers growing tall against the stone cloister leading from the monastery to the chapel. The sunny jonquils looked upward, greeting her as she passed. The purple, white and yellow heads of iris stood tall, claiming a large area of their own where they were free to grow wild with the lilies.

The garden was expansive, with a granite statue of the Virgin Mary in the center flanked by precisely trimmed hedges. Four cobblestone paths led to the center with a resting bench along each path where Sisters often settled in for prayer and meditation. Not on this day, however, as there was much to do to prepare for the feast.

The monastery sat in the north of France, a desired area for politicians and statesmen to meet with and influence wealthy landowners and businessmen of the area. It was unusual for Mother Marie Louise to allow political events on the tranquil grounds of the monastery. However, it had become necessary to provide their real estate and services for a fee. The money offered in exchange for the use of the grounds and buildings and for their service helped to fund the charity work of the monastery.

For nearly a decade since the Sisters harbored Hannah and other Jewish orphans, the Order had been approached to take in local orphans. Hannah's path to the monastery was marred with secrecy, bribery, unimaginable living conditions and suffocating fear. Her parents both lost their lives in the process. Her mother contracted an illness and her father was killed by a lost soul who stole then sold children for forced labor. Hannah's papa died protecting her when they were discovered working in the fields at a farm. Hannah managed to survive when the farmer shot at the would-be abductor, causing him to flee.

The farmer knew it would not be long before Hannah was targeted again now that they discovered her presence. His contacts agreed to get Hannah to refuge with the Sisters at the monastery safely. By the time she reached France, Hannah was an orphaned girl of nine who had seen more horror than most people saw in a lifetime.

The sisters at the monastery were kind to her. Some, like Sister Celeste who had since passed on, were nurturing and comforting as her own Mama was. Others, like Sister Albertine, were stoic and emphasized discipline and learning. As the years passed Hannah grew to love the monastery, the sisters and the friars, and accepted them as family. She did not really have to choose to convert from Judaism to Catholicism as the words and rituals of her upbringing were long forgotten. The safety and routine of the monastery kept fear in check, and she found the scripture filled with hope and comfort.

Hannah spent little time with children her own age in the early years at the monastery. At times she visited the homes of parishioners who had children. They showed her their rooms, filled with dolls, and child-sized furniture. Some would let her touch the porcelain faces of their dolls but others would grab the doll away from her and run to their mamas. This, of course, garnered her a lesson on the sin of coveting from the attending Sister.

The flowers Hannah sought were on the far side of the

garden. She grabbed the snippers and a basket from the stone table in the shade of the chestnut tree and continued on to the wildflower garden, passing the wisteria-adorned stone potting shed. The beauty of the purple wisteria flowers against the grey stone with the occasional splash of bright green moss captured her attention in the early days here. There was something soothing yet haunting in that contrast. God had planted beauty everywhere here, and she could imagine living nowhere else in the world.

Her imagination on the subject, however, was stifled as she had not left the monastery and nearby communities since her arrival. The study of geography at the monastery was lacking, as the nuns had limited experience as well. Having lived her early years in Germany, Hannah was more traveled than the vast majority of them. She once pointed that out when Sister Emily tried to teach the students that Germany was one of the countries in Scandinavia. The lesson quickly turned to one of ill-desired boastful children. Hannah had not corrected a Sister since, although when back in her dormitory room she snickered under her breath at some of the nonsensical things she heard.

In the wildflower garden, brilliant red poppies rose above the white daisies with radiant yellow pompom centers. She clipped some daisies. Daisies were great in arrangements because they were so versatile and went well with the more colorful flowers. She gathered several varieties as she made her way back through the garden. She added a few of the blue love-in-the-mist flowers to the basket as she passed their bed. Those flowers, unlike most of the others in the garden, did not return year after year, but the nuns harvested the seeds and replanted them every year. These were some of the same flowers that grew in her mama's garden in front of their home in Germany.

Hannah did not recall many details of her early life in Berlin, but she remembered the flowers. In the summer Papa frequently plucked a love-in-the-mist blossom and presented it to Mama. He told her that she was as delicate as the lacy leaf of the flower and as bold as the brilliant blue of the blossom. Despite the hardships of those last few months together, her parents loved one another to the bitter end. Papa, once a successful businessman in Berlin and respected by the politicals there, abandoned success without hesitation on that fateful day when the soldiers raided the streets as families gathered for the May Day celebration. One image stayed in her mind from that day: dancing around the Maypole with her friends Sarah and Gertie. Hannah allowed herself to wonder, as she had hundreds of times, if Sarah, also a Jew, had escaped. Gertie and her family, wealthy friends of Papa and Mama, would certainly have survived and continued to live in Berlin. They were not Jews.

In an hour Hannah gathered a basketful of beauty and returned to the washroom to assemble bouquets for the evening. The hour was well spent in reflection and affirmation that she had arrived right where she was meant to be. Her life was simple, yet safe. She was loved and secure and on occasions, like this day, a little extra color came into her world.

The guests arrived shortly before dusk. There were about twenty guests, half of whom would stay in the friar's quarters. The others would return to their homes in the region, escorted by their drivers. After the Sisters served the food, they left the dining hall. They were not privy to the conversations the group of men engaged in. Anna was perfectly comfortable being left out of the conversations. She was not the least bit curious about politics. She retired to the library to study and write.

Hours passed, and before she knew it, the clock had turned to the following day. She heard the assigned Sisters cleaning the dining room and preparing for the following day when they would serve breakfast before the guests departed. She was finishing a final journal entry when a man walked into the study. He sat down in one of the study chairs and engaged her in conversation.

The man introduced himself as Sênior Bevis Rodrigue from Portugal. He inherited land nearby when his mother passed away. He said he enjoyed visiting the area at least annually to get away from his hectic life in Portugal. He inferred that he held a political position there, although Anna did not pursue this further.

When Anna was invited to explain why she was up late in the study, she explained to Sênior Rodrigue her role at the monastery as an apprentice midwife. She had a patient with a rash that they had not been able to heal using the usual salves. She went back to the books and journals to find an alternative. He recited a list of herbs he used in Portugal for similar purposes, some in a tea, and others in a tincture. There were some new combinations that Anna had not attempted with this patient and she was grateful for his knowledge shared.

Sênior Rodrigue noted that Anna's pronunciation and intonation were not purely French, although she was fluent in the language. Sênior Rodrigue was well traveled and extremely well educated. He had business dealings in many countries and was fluent in several languages. He detected a Germanic flair in her pronunciation and word choice. On a hunch, he began conversing in German. After an initial surprise, Hannah reverted to her native language, which she rarely used since starting school under the tutelage of the Sisters. One year she was asked to teach her classmates some basic German language. That was the extent of any conversations using the language in recent years.

Before the first light of dawn emerged, she had described her transition from Berlin, the loss of her family, and life at the monastery. She responded to many questions about the Holocaust and the atrocities against Jews like her family, and other societal "misfits" as they were regarded. In large part Anna had been shielded from news of the war and war-torn Berlin in particular. As with every aspect of her life since arriving at the monastery, she saw the world through Catholic teachings. Sênior Rodrigue quickly realized that due to her young age when taken in by the order and sheltered from such disputes, she did not fear allegations of religious treason.

"Honestly Sênior Rodrigue, I never considered retaliation from the Jews. What I knew growing up with my parents was a happy family without conflict. I was exposed to the Jewish teachings a young child was typically exposed to through Hebrew school and synagogue, as well as the prayer and ritual my family practiced at home. For me, the sense of belonging and the practice of ritual here have allowed me to recreate the security and peace I need in the world. While I may not choose to say this to others, I believe that we each have our own path to Him. Mine was certainly unique, as yours undoubtedly was and continues to be. My tendency is to evaluate the heart and actions of others and not the hours of the day that they pray or whence they were first taught to prayer. The prayers sent up by each of us are unique. Our state of mind and attitude when praying impacts how the prayers are released and received. Perhaps because of my early experiences, I am more tolerant of variety in religious expression. If I were more critical, I fear I would have no faith. After all, as I recall, the Führer was baptized into the Catholic faith."

"May I?" Sênior Rodrigue reached out to take Sister Anna's hand, which she timidly offered. "Your view, dear Sister, is refreshing and I believe necessary for our blessed religion to survive. Your eloquent descriptions and purity of heart are much needed in this world. I can see that you thrive in the shelter of your almost reclusive life, compared to the public life I am forced to live. I do wish you could share your view, if not through public speaking, then through your writings. At the very least, may I take you as a pen pal so we can continue these conversations through ink and paper?"

"That sounds delightful, Sênior Rodrigue. I will have to get the permission of Mother Marie Louise. Leave me your address, please, and if she consents, I will send the first letter."

Sênior Rodrigue was a man who cherished heartfelt conversation and appreciated unique attributes in people over the 'mundane drones', as he called them, that he often encountered. He expressed his delight with their meeting and excused himself for a wink of sleep before breakfast.

20

EDUCATING GERTIE

"Gertrude Hall, I would like to present you with an offer of a lifetime."

The handsome Professor Alex James sat smugly behind his office desk, surrounded by stacks of magazines and piles of manuscripts.

"Is that so, Professor James? Get over here and tell me what you've got." Gertie slapped the sofa next to her.

"Gertie, I'm serious. You've been a wonderful lab assistant this past year but I think it's about time you get some experience in the field."

"Just what did you have in mind, Alex? You know I've got experience in the field, the canoe, your kitchen table. Just where would you like to take me now?"

Professor James stood and came around the desk toward the sofa. He turned back to grab a letter from the top of a pile on the desk.

"You're going to want to thank me for this Ms. Hall. I mean REALLY thank me for this." He leaned into Gertie, kissed her cheek and handed her the letter before walking to the door. He turned the lock until a solid click sounded, like he had done dozens of times in recent months with Gertie securely inside and pesky graduate students kept at bay.

———————

GERTIE STARTED her studies at the London University with a full load of sciences and literature. Unsure of what she ultimately wanted to become, she drifted toward those subjects that intrigued her most. Late in the second year she attended a symposium featuring a number of physical scientists and social scientists. For the entire week Gertie sat through lecture after lecture, learning about new theories, research and field studies. The French anthropologist, Dina Dreyfus, who had studied the Bororo Indian tribes in the Amazon Rainforest, made one late afternoon presentation. Gertie was spellbound with the stories of discovery and surveillance. She listened to other anthropologists as well as archeologists and sociologists. She captured their theories in notes about the study of race and society. As that school year wound down, she returned to those notes time and again to review and try to reconcile the different theories she had heard during the presentations. "To determine race in an anthropologic sense, we must examine the biological traits of a population" versus "Race reflects the cultural values and religious beliefs of a people" versus "Biologic characteristics be damned; it's the social world that defines race".

The world of anthropology became Gertie's first true love affair. She mapped out courses, saturating her class schedule with Theory of Anthropology, Ethnography of West Africa, Ethnography of South East Asia, Anthropology of Gender, and Principles of Social Investigation. She spent the summer in the University library reading every text she could find written by an anthropologist.

In the fall of her third year Gertie set an appointment with the esteemed head of the anthropology department, Professor Alex James. She had read articles written by and about

Professor James and was prepared to have an in-depth discussion with him about social anthropology, his area of specialty. A handsome man in his mid-forties greeted her. Graying hair appeared to be swept back from his face by the wind, yet the air was still. A broad smile and glasses gave him a distinguished look. He was fairly tall with a sturdy, muscular build, unlike the thin, pale-faced mathematics professors she had encountered or the rotund, red-faced literature professors.

Gertie introduced herself and they spent the next two hours talking about the professor's various publications and some of his field studies. Finally, they got to the ultimate reason for Gertie's visit. "When I sit back and look at people and hear of cultures, it strikes me that there are far more similarities than differences between populations. I think we are so entrenched in our mission to find something new and different—to make discoveries—that we discard the notion of similarity. The real skill, the art here, is to explain our sameness so that we can be united and extinguish divisiveness of races. We all know that each grain of sand is different, but collectively they are the same and provide us a firm foundation to plant our feet on. The same is true of snow. Each snowflake is different, but they all act the same and serve the same purpose. Many people believe I am a feminist because I choose to speak my mind and use my voice, but why do I have to be labeled anything? I do not advocate as a woman wanting what a man has. I am a human walking beside, co-existing with and integrating with, other humans."

"Ms. Hall, yours is exactly the alternative thought we are looking for in our graduate program. As you know, we have a regimented program that requires you to study popular philosophers and implement established study protocols; however, with your alternative view of the world you could study the same subjects and have an entirely different set of data and hypothesis. Should you elect to pursue a graduate degree, I would welcome the opportunity to challenge you in my program."

Over the next few years Gertie saw Professor James in passing and exchanged small talk. She caught his attention again well into the second year of her graduate program when she applied for PhD studies and a graduate assistantship. The application process required a panel interview, led by Professor James. Gertie's clever wit, passion, vast knowledge and raw, fresh ideals impressed the panel. Professor James prodded with inquiries that highlighted her areas of interest and aptitude.

Gertie made a point of visiting his office in the week following the interview. She stood in the doorway to speak to him. "Thank you, Professor James."

"Miss Hall, I wondered just how long it would take you to stop by. I think the panel was quite impressed with you."

"How could they not be? You paved the way nicely with your questions. Do you do that for all of your applicants?"

"I take special interest in those with the most promise."

"You think I have promise then?"

"Miss Hall, you offer more promise than the book of Matthew." With that they both laughed and Gertie turned to walk away. "Miss Hall, I DO look forward to seeing you back here in the fall. We'll discuss your teaching assistant assignment then."

Gertie met with pals at the bar that night. School was winding down for the year. A Master's Degree would soon be in her hand, and the future looked bright. To celebrate and satisfy hormonal desires, she went home with an acquaintance from the bar. She emerged from his flat two days later with a smile on her face and feeling free as a bird. The world of anthropology was hers to conquer.

Gertie secured a job for the summer as a gopher at a local newspaper. It had been a big year for the news, and the business was flush. There were headlines of Elvis Presley's rise in the music scene and Marilyn Monroe's persona makeover. The summer Olympics were coming. British troops and British Rail were always good for a headline or two. It would not be glamorous work but she would meet people, let her hair down some after six hard years of study, and make some pocket money. She looked forward to integrating into the world outside academia.

A stranger to no one, Gertie met a number of interesting people that summer. One woman in particular brought a new perspective to her world. During one of their late night, whiskey lubricated discussions this new friend posed a series of questions that resonated with Gertie.

"What if we each knew our souls and our purpose here on earth? Do we really need to knock one another down and climb on each other's backs, as a neighbor, as a city, and even as nations? If war and elitism were wiped out from our arsenals of superiority wouldn't we be a happier people?"

Abigail Bradley lived an authentic life. She was a married mother of modest means who loved her roles as wife and mother but had not given up her passion for self expression, even in the harshest of economies. Gertie met Abigail one weekend while at the market to retrieve staples. Abigail was drawing portraits in a side room of the local market next to a pub. She did not charge for these portraits, but accepted items in trade. Abigail's portraits were not ordinary drawings. She incorporated backgrounds that were intuited. Invariably the recipient of the portraits had a special connection to the scene or shadows forming the frame of the portrait. Abigail drew Gertie. Central to the picture was a smiling, carefree Gertie. In the background there were one hundred faces looking in all directions. Some faces were familiar to Gertie. Her mother, father and a few others from her youth looked back at her. Each face was unique. Gertie shivered when she looked into the faces. "They are all part of me and I of them. I am their voice where they have none."

Gertie was a magnet for people who fell outside the mainstream, which was part of her gift. She saw the world from a different center of normal and often furrowed her brow as she tried to understand her peers' perspectives on life, religion, and politics. She strained so much that she developed a permanent crease above her nasal bridge, contributing to a mature and wise appearance. But it was the brilliant smile and keen wit that drew people to her. She was a comforting soul for many who had difficulty relating to the norm.

Over the next several years Gertie and Professor Alex James spent many hours together. She was an assistant in the department, but not exclusively for him. As Gertie threw herself into academia, he found every opportunity he could to introduce her to the public. Gertie often accompanied Alex to public speaking engagements and after-hours fundraisers throughout the city. She was always presented as his student, never as a date. On these occasions, however, they frequently spent the entire night together. Both unmarried, they enjoyed one another's company. Alex was divorced from an archeologist who needed to relocate several years prior to further her career, at a time when Alex was driven to pursue academia. Their divorce was natural and amicable.

Initially Gertie and Alex found themselves waxing on prophetically about theory, but eventually they discovered a mutual passion for the physical release found in a somewhat athletic sexual romp. By Gertie's final year in the program, they had fallen into a rhythm. Each knew they weren't in an exclusive relationship but had the comfort of knowing the other was always there in a detached, comfortable way. This was the year for Gertie to conduct an extended field study to finalize her dissertation, and Alex took a sabbatical to accompany her.

Alex's former wife, Olivia, was leading an archeological dig on Puna Island in the Gulf of Guayaquil. She invited Alex to partner on an academic paper, integrating her study of migrating agrarian culture of the Colonial Formative period with biological attributes of the inhabitants. With Olivia's blessing, Alex arranged for Gertie to do her extended field study as a part of this excursion. Gertie's contributions to the study from a socio-cultural aspect, particularly in a country that was not undergoing radical gender shifts based on modern-day political decisions, would be invaluable. As for furthering Gertie's education, Alex knew that confronting Gertie with hypotheses that challenged her innate view of the world as uniform, without gender distinctions, brought out the best critical analysis. On this project, she could make her mark and challenge customary thought in the field of anthropology.

Initially, Gertie was hesitant with the proposed area of study. Curiosity about Olivia, however, got the best of her. As she understood it, Olivia and Alex had split because of professional endeavors. Alex was open about his continuing communications with Olivia and always spoke of her with a nostalgic, wishful tone.

More than anything, Gertie looked forward to putting her education to work. Bored with academia and eager to make her mark on the world, she immersed herself in the preparations. She dispersed her meager collection of secondhand furniture and housewares, asked a friend to store texts and packed the few essentials she thought she needed. They were limited in the amount of cargo they could take, as part of that space was committed to items requested by Olivia for her team's supplies.

They arrived in Quito, Ecuador on an unusually hot day in May. The journey had taken two weeks, and they were both exhilarated and exhausted. The dig party welcomed them and the first day was spent getting acquainted with one another and the project.

The group was an interesting mix of academics, a philanthropist with a keen interest in the area, Ecuadorian government staff and others who performed manual labor that kept the camp running. The friendships Gertie made here would last her lifetime. The experience had a profound and unanticipated impact on both her personal and professional growth. An entry in Gertie's journal written several months into the field study captured her observations.

Minds, hands and souls unite as we work under the heat of the sun and in the pelting rain. Each of us a voyeur into the lives of ancient peoples, picking apart various aspects of their homes, culture, family, and spiritual life. Then, when we come together after a long day in the field, we assemble our interpretations. Mythology, spirituality, art and science meld as we give meaning to the parts and assemble the whole. Olivia is a mastermind at introducing mythos and culture as a construct for understanding daily life. Each unearthed potsherd, figurine, bola stone, trench, wall, stair, etc. has a function and comparable item in the present day. These familiar objects show me how homogenous the human race is. Our similarities over the centuries are astounding.

21

SALLY'S CONFESSION

When Sally was young nightmares were common, but as an adult they appeared only when she was under a lot of stress. Pregnancy induced more nightmares. One night was particularly frightening for both of them. George held Sally as she flailed in her sleep, crying out, "Papa! Papa! Bitte nicht schießen sie, Papa!"

Sally trembled with fear as she awakened. She was drenched with sweat in the late summer heat and disheveled from thrashing. The nightmares had returned even before her body showed signs of their developing baby.

George feared this pregnancy was too much for her. "Sal, they seem to be getting worse. Isn't there something the doctor can do to help you with these nightmares?"

George didn't like being woken by cries and thrashing; but more than anything, it was Sally he was worried about. For him, it was just an inconvenience. For her, it was becoming a health issue. If she did not get some relief before school started, he didn't know how she could return to the teaching job she loved so much.

Sally sat up and took a drink of water from the glass on the nightstand. She wondered what she had cried out this time.

George told her she spoke in a foreign language when she had nightmares; German, he thought. She told him her mother made her stop speaking German when they moved to America. The truth was, she spoke German fluently, and when she and her mother were alone, she enjoyed speaking in their native language.

Sally wiped her eyes with the back of her hand and turned to George, bracing for the look of pity and worry she would find there. "Meet me in the kitchen, we need to talk."

She peed and changed her sopping wet nightgown. She found George at the table in the kitchen with a fresh glass of water poured for each of them. Sally opened the kitchen door to let some fresh air in, sat down and drank the glass of water in one continuous drink. She dreaded this conversation, but knew she had to have it.

"George, these nightmares are not from being pregnant. I have had them since I was a little girl. They went away when I went to college, unless I was under a lot of stress. There are some things I have to tell you. I think you need to know about my childhood before we bring a child into this world. I don't know if it will make the nightmares stop, but I hope so."

George got up and pulled a pitcher of water from the icebox. He poured them each a fresh glass and sat back down across from Sally. He was confused about references to Sally's childhood. He knew she was from Denmark, then New York, and was raised by her mother and uncle after her father died. Nothing could have prepared him for the story about to unfold.

"You met and married me, Sally Fischer. You know I came from Denmark with my mother as a young girl. George, you must forgive me. Promise you will forgive me for not telling you what I am preparing to tell you. You will understand when I am done, but you must promise me."

"Sal, I promise. I promise, you could do nothing I could not forgive." He took her hand in his and kissed it gently.

"I was born a German-Jew. My father, Ira Fischel, was a

professor at a university in Berlin. A music professor. We lived in an elite area of Berlin when I was born, where German-Catholics and German-Jews existed side by side. My friends and schoolmates were Jewish and non-Jewish alike. Father was well liked and often invited, along with his students, to perform at municipal and military functions and for the families of the wealthy in the area."

Sally shifted in her chair and took another long drink of water. It had been a long time since she reminisced about those happier early years.

"Papa was older than Mama. She had been one of his students. They fell madly in love. She dropped out of school when they married. My brother, Isaac, was born their second year of marriage and I just a year later. Mama and Papa had friends all over the city and were very involved in the arts. Music seemed to bring much color into our home, both in the variety of music we listened to and in the assortment of people who stopped in."

"It was an idyllic life when I was young, it really was. I remember having tea parties and I went to school with my best friends Hannah and Gertie. We were the female version of the three musketeers. We were inseparable. We made plans to grow up and travel the world together before we married and had babies of our own."

"Life was good for us until the Jews and others came under attack in Berlin. Papa felt safe and felt our family was safe early on, but then things changed at the university. He was removed from his position because of his Jewish faith. He was still called upon to arrange entertainment and we had plenty of money so we did not need to move. My papa had inherited a good deal of money from his father, who was a businessman with dealings in a number of countries. That diversity proved very important when things got bad in Germany. I'm sorry I never got to meet my Opa."

Sally stood and walked to the screen door. She flicked at a

moth that had landed there, not hard enough to make it fly away, just enough to let it know she was there. She started talking again as she moved to the counter and leaned her back against its edge.

"We saw less and less of our friends and neighbors until one spring everything changed. I think I knew that things were changing in Berlin, but I was pretty sheltered. I still went to the same school, but the school days were shorter and there were fewer older boys in school those days. Gertie and Hannah were there, so my world still seemed pretty normal. I remember talking about the May Day celebration coming up. Every year we went to the parade and then to the park. That year, Papa had told us that we could not go to the parade and the Maypole dance. He said that instead, we were going to spend the rest of the day near the synagogue with the other Jewish families on the recommendation of the rabbi."

Sally sat back down at the table across from George. "That's when everything changed. It seems like we were forced to make a decision to stand united with our Jewish family, against the German culture we lived in. Tensions had grown enough that we avoided being out after dark. Anyway, we did get to go to the May Day celebration after all. My friend Gertie's father, Mr. Hall, stopped by and invited us to join their family at the May Day festival. He said that he was reminding the whole neighborhood about the events and that my friend Hannah's family would also be joining. Mr. Hall was a military officer so Papa and Mama thought it would be okay to go. My parents had talked to us some about the fact that one day we may need to leave Berlin to a safer place. I later learned that my father had secretly gotten documents changing our names, so we could get out of the country if we needed to."

Sally paused again to take in some fresh water and adjust herself in the chair. George no longer sat back in his chair. He was leaning forward, elbows on the table, looking intently at his wife as she shared her story. A tight knot formed in the pit of his stomach.

"I remember that we did not go to the May Day parade. Papa was on edge. We danced in the parlor, like we did so many days. Sometimes it was for only a few minutes and other times the dancing went on for hours. Papa said that music was necessary. It spoke to our heart, our souls, and our bodies in ways that just words could not. He would say, 'music is love floating in the air.'

"Papa told us it was almost time to go. He sent me up to get my sweater and Isaac to make sure the windows were all closed and locked. That was something he had started doing in the weeks before that day. Mama went to the kitchen to get the picnic basket. I remember we were all ready and waiting for Papa in the kitchen so we could leave, but he wasn't there. Then I saw him racing down the stairs with a suitcase. He went outside. I heard the car door slam, then he was back in the kitchen and we all left."

The list of follow-up questions was forming in George's mind, but he did not want to interrupt her story. He stretched his legs out releasing the tension some but sat perched on the edge of the chair waiting for Sally to continue.

"We got to the park before the parade ended. The park wasn't crowded yet, and the Maypole dancing was just getting started. There was a little community band setting up to play the music, and mothers were taking their younger children to the streamers coming from the pole and demonstrating how they should walk. That year was about my third year to dance, if I remember right." A hint of a smile showed at the edges of Sally's lips.

"Isaac and I each grabbed a ribbon and lined up. Gertie and Hannah ran up from the parade and joined in. A couple of Isaac's friends were there too, and other children we knew from school. The music started and we danced around the pole. It was a large Maypole with two rows of children, one inside the other. The row closest to the pole went one direction, and the outer row went the opposite direction. When we passed our friends, we would clap hands or the boys would give each other a little shove. We had fun. Come to think of it, I don't think I've ever seen this here in the States. Anyway, we danced several dances and then had a picnic. Mama always packed the best picnics, and that day she had a special little cake for each of us. Oh my, I don't believe I remember that. We were just finishing our picnic when Papa told us it was time to go. Gertie was gone, and I had lost sight of Hannah. A lot of people had come from the parade by that time and it was a bit chaotic, I think."

Sally paused, and searched her memory for that moment, when they packed up the picnic blanket. It was faded, and she couldn't retrieve it completely. She remembered that the picnic blanket was blue and white. Her father had a worried face and wanted them to hurry.

"We walked between houses on the way home and didn't stay on the street. I thought it was strange, but Papa was rushing us and wanted us to keep up with him. Mama held my hand and smiled down at me. My mother is one brave woman. She loved and trusted my papa completely. We followed Papa right to the car. We never went back into the house. I fell asleep and woke up as it was getting dark. When I stepped out of the car, I stepped into straw. We had parked in a barn. Boy, did it smell. Papa got our bags out of the trunk, and someone was there with a lantern. They showed us a little room where they kept saddles and things at the end of the barn. The wall with the tack hanging on it was kind of a trick wall. You couldn't see a door handle, but it opened up and inside were four cots and a chamber pot. There were blankets on the cots and there was some fruit and something else to eat. I don't remember now what it was. We stayed in that little room, quiet as church mice, for a few days. Each day the man or the woman of the house brought us food. We were able to step out into the barn for a short time each day, but not for very long. Our car was moved somewhere."

"After a few days a big farm truck pulled into the barn one night. When we heard it pull up, we got very quiet. I'm sure I was holding my breath. The farmer came to let us out of the room, and as we came out we saw two families crawl out of different places of that truck. It was set up to look like it was hauling farm stuff, like milk and eggs and chickens, maybe even produce, I don't remember, but there were different hiding places. We were told where our hiding places would be and soon everyone was on the truck and it was going down the road. Before we got on, Papa had us put on an extra layer of clothes and he tucked papers in our clothes. Papa told us some secret things, like how old we were and our new pretend names. He tried to make a game of it but it didn't seem fun. I wasn't too happy about crawling into an old crate, but knew I didn't have a choice. Then he told us that when we felt scared, we could sing songs in our head and he named some happy songs that we knew. 'Nobody can take away your happy songs,' he said."

Sally stopped. She drew in a deep breath and turned away, wiping tears that had welled up in her eyes. "I have to use the bathroom. I'll be right back."

George stepped outside and drew in the night air in a long breath. He felt sick to his stomach and his thoughts were racing. His beautiful wife, a hidden Jew. How did he not know this? How did she survive? Thank God she survived! Sally was sitting back down at the table with some juice and a couple of Saltines when he returned.

"Sal." George wanted her to stop, if she needed to. They could pick up from here tomorrow. He knew she needed some sleep.

"George, no, let me finish. This all seems so surreal now, but really, I need to finish. Come. Come sit with me." George obliged, feeling too ill to eat or drink anything.

"One of the couples had a baby. It was crying, and the mother could not comfort it. She handed it to the farmer's wife and got back on the truck and into her hiding place. I just cannot imagine leaving your baby behind. I would die first before I could do that." Sally paused for a drink, washing down the lump of emotions stuck in her throat.

"Once we were all loaded onto the truck, a heavy duck cloth went over the top. It was stifling inside that box under the tarp. Once the truck started, I could no longer hear the sobs of the mother. I don't know if she stopped crying or the noise of the truck drowned out the sound. I remember being curled up inside that crate feeling as if I was going to crawl out of my skin. I played one of those songs over and over in my head, just like Papa had said. I don't know how long we were on that truck. It felt like days, but I hadn't wet myself so it must have been hours. I had heard somebody say something about Denmark, but at the time I didn't really understand what that meant."

"Apparently, we would not be going into Denmark but to a farm close to the border where we could then easily make our way over the border. The truck ran into a roadblock with German soldiers who were searching the vehicles stopped there. I can't really describe the chaos that followed with much detail, but I do remember that the soldiers unloaded everything on that truck and found us. They drug us off that truck; put the women and girls on one side of the road and the men and boys on the other side. I don't know why, but Papa had given Mama his papers to hold, and he never took them back from her. I think it was when he was talking to Isaac and I and putting our papers in our clothing that he asked her to hold them and then never took them back. Anyway, when the soldiers asked Papa for his papers, he didn't have them. Mama tried to give them to the soldier, but they wouldn't let her. The soldiers taunted Papa and told he and the other men to run for the border and if they could outrun the bullets, they could live.

He and other men that were lined up at the road block started running. Papa did not make it. We watched them shoot him and there was nothing we could do. My brother was marched onto a truck with other boys and some women and girls who did not have papers. Mother showed the soldiers our papers and they let us walk up the road. Mama was singing quietly under her breath to keep both of us from becoming hysterical, I think. At the time I thought it absolutely ridiculous that she would be singing then, but looking back on it, it was one of the most heroic things she could have done."

Sally paused again, feeling as if she had just run an emotional marathon telling her story. She was not done though and needed to finish. She needed to get to safety and not leave herself hanging in that horrific moment when her father was killed and her brother taken away, never to be seen again.

"I don't know why those soldiers let us go. We walked, with about six or seven other women and children, in the lights of the roadblock. One of the women had a map of sorts that showed where we were to go. It was off the main road, so we veered off the road once we were out of sight of the soldiers. It was dark, so we stayed fairly close to the road until we got to a turnoff marked on the map. We walked through the night and into the day. When we heard a vehicle, we threw ourselves into the shrubs and tall grass. By mid-morning we could see the farmhouse marked on the map. We were exhausted, frightened, and hungry but did not want to go up to the door. Instead, we lay in the grass, watching to see if there were any soldiers around. Finally, one of the older girls got up and ran for the farmhouse. She knocked on the door and a man answered. A little while later we were all fed and cleaned up. There was a rural area where we could cross over a bridge into Denmark. We had the name and address of a mission service on the other side that would help us when we crossed over. We didn't rest, but kept on going. We were all in need of safety at that point. Really, looking back, I think if we had stopped, some of the women who had lost their husbands and sons would not be able to keep going."

"Once in Denmark, we went to that mission service that contacted the Jewish rescue group that helped us find a place to stay. We stayed in Denmark for almost a year, trying, through the underground, to locate my brother. We were told that healthy German-Jewish children were put to work in labor camps or were used for medical experiments. After a year, when we could not locate him and it was clear that we could not return to Berlin, my mother contacted her brother, Uncle Morris, who had moved to the United States. Our contacts in Denmark helped pay for our passage, and we sailed to New York. While on the ship, my mother made me promise that our life would start over once we got to the United States. We agreed to never talk about what happened. I was so young, but still understood the magnitude of what she was saying. She also said we would never stop looking for Isaac. When we immigrated, we changed our last name from Fischel to Fischer and my given name of Sarah was changed to Sally. Every year Mama wrote to all the Jewish rescue groups she could find to learn anything she could of my brother, but we have never had any answers. I can imagine that if he survived, he is doing something very honorable, like becoming a doctor. Every year on May Day my mother sits in prayer. She says that was the day the darkness came and changed her life. Other than that, she does not practice any religion now. When we immigrated, we were identified as Lutherans because we came from Denmark. We left everything Jewish behind and for my mother, that has been difficult for her to reconcile."

George sat across from this amazing woman, telling this horribly tragic story of love and loss. Tears were streaming down his face. What a brave child she was. What horrific secrets she has held as promised. For a long while they sat in silence, holding hands, processing the story and the images that unfolded across the kitchen table.

"George, I need to sleep."

"Yes, of course, let's get some rest."

Exhausted, they fell into bed, wrapped in the warm blanket of the dark night. Morning came and passed before they awoke from a long overdue restorative slumber.

22

HANNAH THE PRACTITIONER

Not long after Sister Anna began making house calls on her own, she had an experience that shook her to the core. After years of trying, a local couple in their mid-thirties had conceived a child. They referred to the anticipated baby as their 'miracle child' and joyously shared the news of this blessing with family and friends. Anna was aware of the pregnancy but not consulted to provide care as the village doctor was following the couple.

One night, after days of heavy rainfall and flash flooding, a frantic rap on the door awakened Sister Anna. The expectant woman had fallen down some stone steps on their property and lay in the rain for some time before being found. The flooding washed out the bridge leading to town and the nearest doctor. Anna was able to reach the home through back roads and footbridges. The woman was in heavy labor by the time she arrived. She was only seven months pregnant and had suffered a serious blow to the head. She was conscious, but in pain and severely ill.

The baby arrived after a couple hours of labor. He was tiny and obviously deformed. The new mother bled heavily after the delivery and was too weak to take tea to help control the bleeding. She soon lost consciousness. The husband lay with her and the baby boy until he stopped breathing, shortly after birth.

Covered in blood from trying to stop the hemorrhage using every method she could devise, Sister Anna advised the husband that his wife was unlikely to make it. If there were any chance at all for survival, she would have to get to a hospital for surgery to remove her uterus. There was no traversable route to get her there. She slipped away soon after, joining her son in the afterlife. Anna had witnessed many deaths from trauma and disease, but never before felt so helpless to bring comfort to the dying or the living.

"I am the resurrection and the life. The one who believes in me will live, even though they die; and whoever lives by believing in me will never die." (John 11:25-26) The words repeated in her mind but did not bring solace to her shaken soul. On returning to the monastery she entered three days of silence, praying for guidance and comfort. When she emerged, she spent time with Sister Marie, reviewing what she did and what more she could have done. Sister Marie assured her she had done everything possible. "God calls us home when he needs us, not when we and others are ready."

Years of prayer and surrender passed before Sister Anna released this experience. In many ways it seemed easier for her to reconcile the loss of her parents than this expectant mother who was in her care. Finally, she realized that her sense of control was less developed as a young child. Now, after years of study, she wanted to control the outcomes for the patients in her care. During many evenings with Sister Marie, she explored the realities of their obligations to care for the sick and dying, the poor and disadvantaged. In addition, hours and days were spent in prayer to surrender the need to control. Cognitively, she was well aware that she could not overpower

God's will; nonetheless, the tendency was to care too much about the outcome. Acceptance of God's hand in the prognosis for patients eventually came, although there were times when she would have liked to take on the argument with the good Lord himself.

23

GERTIE MOVES ON

Gertie enjoyed the fieldwork in Ecuador and gathered enough material to draft her dissertation. The final body of work proved to be more interesting than she initially thought it would be. Her relationship with the handsome professor changed. It became clear to Gertie that he and his former bride still had deep feelings for one another. The palpable but unspoken sexual tension between Alex and Olivia played out in the bedroom that Gertie shared with Alex. It manifested as raw sexual drive.

Alex's sexual appetite became insatiable. Initially, this new level of energy excited Gertie, but when she confronted him, his affection turned romantic. Until then, romance had never been a part of their relationship. Their attraction was founded on academic passion and physical lust, but detached from the usual hopes and dreams of growing old together. Gertie's response was to bury herself in work. She became unavailable to receive Alex's affections. Initially, excuses included quiet time to complete her dissertation but once that was done, the excuses expanded to include trips for supplies and time to conduct observations in locations inconvenient to returning nightly. More than once she slept on the couch of a co-worker, swearing them to be silent about her presence.

After a few months of this dance, Gertie accepted Alex's invitation for a romantic evening that he planned. Gertie arranged, through slight deception, to have Olivia attend instead. As predicted, alone with music playing, wine flowing and lights dimmed, Olivia and Alex's bottled attraction was uncorked and within hours they were entwined in each other's welcoming limbs.

Comparing notes, they quickly and correctly surmised that Gertie had arranged for their reunion. Any sense of guilt quickly dissipated, and they lost themselves in their reunion.

After hours of rekindling a passion that had never completely been extinguished, the couple turned the conversation to Gertie. She had given them a gift, and they wanted to respond in kind. Drunk on love, filled with gratitude and too excited to sleep, they devised a plan to introduce Gertie to some of the most influential people in anthropology that they knew. These were the individuals who could assist with launching her career. They both agreed that she had the expansive and eccentric thought and immense drive that could someday make her a big name in the field. They drafted a list of ten influential contacts, assembling a mix of financiers and scholarly icons.

During the night Gertie composed her own list—a list of future accomplishments and places to travel. The list started with a trip to visit her mother. Gertie had not seen her mother since she left home at seventeen those many years before. She felt a pull to visit her. Also listed were three remote areas of the world to visit, five people she wanted to meet, two publications she wanted to write for and one last huge goal: to "shred all human thoughts of racial elitism and reform human relations to eliminate the concept of race." That final goal would drive everything she did from that moment forward.

The private farewell between Alex and Gertie extended

over two days. When Gertie returned to their shared quarters, Alex was dressed and drinking tea alone in the sitting room. Olivia had gone to work, making space for Alex and Gertie to talk. Before he could speak, Gertie handed him her completed dissertation and asked that he look through it while she packed her things.

"I dedicate this dissertation to my mentor, Professor Alex James, a profoundly passionate student of life, teacher of fact, and mystic who, beyond teaching me, has shown me that deep within each of us lies a truth waiting to be birthed and introduced to the world. My truth, as born out through observational research and literature search is that you, reader, regardless of your origin or appearance, are my brethren and when harm comes to you in the name of racial superiority, the culprit brings harm to all, harm that cannot be satisfied by return of property or monetary reward.

In furtherance of this thesis, 'Theoretical Extinction of Racial Superiority through Biophysical Anthropologic Demonstration' is foundational evidence that humans are more alike than different and connected in a greater energetic mass than is currently considered. It is also a platform for further research and my life's purpose to establish that harm brought to one group of people is harm brought to all and that we can celebrate, rather than fear, indigenous ethnic eccentricities. It is fear, not biology, that creates the desire to overcome a race and that fear, being something other than reality, shall be confronted and excised. The people shall be spared."

Gertie took her time packing, placing only those few things she really needed into her luggage and piling the remainder into sorted heaps for the team that remained on site. She packed her notebooks and the few photos taken during the time in Ecuador. She reflected on the images of the locals and the discoveries at the ruin site, and the small collection of mementos given to her by those she had worked with and interviewed. Gently, she placed the most treasured items in the suitcase, including drawings from children, a handmade doll and a small woven cloth.

By the time she finished sorting, packing and tidying up the small quarters, Alex had read large portions of the dissertation. Much of it he had seen earlier, but he was moved by the finality of the project and the competence Gertie demonstrated in her work. He knew that she would surpass him in quantity and quality of work in their shared field. He had become her mentor and mystic and would remain a confidant as she forged new areas of thought and collaboration.

Gertie shared with Alex the plans to visit her mother. He knew this was a big step for her, but no longer sensed the dread that usually permeated the air when she mentioned her mother.

"I'm sure she will be thrilled to see you. How long has it been now?"

"It's been a decade since I saw her. We exchange letters on major holidays and birthdays, but it really has taken me all this while to desire to see her again. This dig, our work… it has given me a renewed appreciation for the societal importance of family, and I have some unanswered questions I need to explore with her."

"Don't be too hard on her. She must be an old woman by now."

"No, no, I won't. Truth be known, I gained many gifts from my mother, not the least of which is the independence I developed through her benign neglect."

"Well now, that doesn't sound too flattering. You will break it to her more gently than that, I hope." They laughed together. Alex used to tease Gertie about her brutally honest proclamations. What Gertie simply thought was telling the truth sounded like harsh judgment to the unwary audience. She did not realize that her truth was not everyone's truth. Over the years together, her edge had softened. She had become socially and politically astute.

Alex presented Gertie with the list of names he and Olivia had compiled. He shared the rationale for each name that was selected. He explained their professional backgrounds and some personal information that would smooth the way to an introduction when the time came. Alex assured Gertie that he held her in the highest esteem as a professional and cherished their personal relationship. They talked about their time together and shared memories. They held each other through the night and made arrangements for Gertie's departure the following day.

After saying goodbye to the locals she had come to know and to the dig party, she embraced Olivia and Alex one last time. Each had tears in their eyes and smiles on their faces.

She departed, ready for the next adventure.

24

WARMTH AND COLOR FOR ANNA

Anna's first letter to Sênior Rodrigue provided a look at a day in the life of Sister Anna at the monastery. Mother Marie Louise agreed to the pen pal exchange on the condition that she, as the Mother Superior, read all outgoing and incoming letters. After several letters passed in each direction and she saw the innocuous nature of the correspondence, the censorship requirement was lifted.

In subsequent letters, Sister Anna described her work as a healer and spiritual awakening. She described an unforgiving pelvis that, with herbs, prayer, and exercises, was coaxed to relinquish the new life trapped within. Some of the most interesting observations she shared were those of terminal patients who recalled their lives, regrets, accomplishments, fears and hopes. She made it her goal with each of those patients to give them dignity and nurture peace within. She felt successful in this area.

Sênior Rodrigue told stories of his travels, business ventures and ultimately, details of his private life. He revealed that he was a homosexual man. He was in a long-time relationship with his assistant but had to maintain a professional facade given his stature in Portugal.

He wrote of the dignitaries he met worldwide and shared his perspectives on religion, humanity and kept her apprised of Jewish reparations activities. In later years, he wrote about a woman he met who was destined to impact world peace in profoundly positive ways. Her work stretched worldwide and was based in science. She had spoken at the United Nations and raised millions of dollars to support her work.

Through the letters, Sister Anna and Sênior Rodrigue exchanged healing discoveries, new uses for herbs and stories of healing they had witnessed or heard of. Sister Anna was so honored to have found kinship with a total stranger. She prayed for him daily.

When Sênior Rodrigue returned to the region, he always made time to visit the monastery and Sister Anna, if she was not away on a house call. On his last trip to the area in his eighties, his longtime assistant and lover, Sébastien, accompanied him. They no longer were forced to live a secret life. Sister Anna found Sébastien to be a kindly, neurotic, humorous soul.

That last trip brought another great surprise as well: a reunion with a friend from her youth.

25

REACHING FOR RECONCILIATION

On the train to Lisbon Gertie reflected on the visit with Mother. She had become a shell of her once-vibrant self, yet there was a sense of peace about her. Having outlived two husbands and losing three homes, she was living with cousins in a rural area of Germany. Her mind was still sharp, but her body was eroding. Gertie was certain this was their last visit, but it seemed that Gertie acquired her nurturing inclinations from her mother. She was not compelled to stay on and care for her.

They spent time reminiscing about Gertie's early days. Her mother had little memory of Gertie's teen years, a combination of lack of engagement with Gertie during that time, a reaction to the trauma of the time, and an age-related memory problem. She had clear memories of Gertie as a small child and shared details about Gertie's father that Gertie was not familiar with. He was a statesman first and foremost. Appearances were critical for him. Her mother spoke of the need for a pristine living environment and fashionable, yet conservative dress for the family, with meticulous grooming.

For the first time, she shared the story of her father's breakdown before his death. One night he returned from an assignment that took him several hours southwest of Berlin. He was sullen and distant. He had lost weight, and aged years in the few weeks he was gone. Gertie and her mother had heard stories about concentration camps and wanted him to share what he knew, but he would not engage. He took to bed for two days, and during that time Gertie's mother often found him sobbing. He would not reveal what had struck him to become dumb and so sullen. That was his last trip home. Within weeks he returned to his post and died. Gertie's mother, in retrospect, surmised that he had killed himself, a fact that would have been buried with his body rather than be confessed by the army.

Gertie had come to despise her father in the years after his death. The more she learned about the Holocaust, the more she hated him. This new revelation, if true, did not excuse his involvement in the massacre under the name of racial superiority, but it did reveal a more humane side which she was previously oblivious to. Another casualty of a senseless racial war based on false premise and fear. Her mother, likewise, was a casualty. The vitality was drained from her as she lost her identity and purpose. She was bred and groomed to be a wife and mother. The war took that away, caused her to lose hope and extinguished her passion. Gertie would not be a victim. She was the daylight that eventually comes after the dark night, bringing new color and meaning to the life created therein. At least she aspired to become so.

The victims of Hitler's regime, she realized, extended beyond those who lost their lives in death camps. It extended to the Jews, homosexuals, gypsies and others whose lives were spared, but forever changed as they lost their possessions, family and friends, home, and everything they had come to know. Gertie reflected on the brutal acts used to strip the presumed inferiors from every element of dignity and essence personified. For the first time in her memory, Gertie wept. She wept for strangers, communities, and for her parents. She did not weep for herself. She felt a power rising within her; a power to confront distorted thinking and barbaric human behaviors.

Gertie had followed news of the Korean War, a short but bloody war. To her it seemed a war for power and control; a war to prove one ideology was superior to another. She accepted that there would always be dark masterminds willing to wage war in the name of something: religion, power, or economic control. What she struggled with were the followers. She contemplated the reasons armies and whole nations supported war. She wrote out a list of reasons and they fell into four categories: economic survival, camaraderie, power/powerlessness, and fear.

She thought about why her papa followed Hitler. He had no professional credentials such as a lawyer or a doctor. His father was a military man, and she knew he was largely influenced by her Opa. Her papa wanted to please his papa and provide for his family the way his own father had. Even if he disagreed with the controlling Nazis, he may have believed he had no option but to stay employed to meet his family's needs.

She realized the price her papa paid for his choice to follow the regime. Ultimately, it cost him his life and along the way he sacrificed the relationship with family, relinquished personal mores and surrendered his voice for humanity. Gertie knew her papa as a strong man in her early childhood. He ruled the household in a firm but loving way. Family and God were important to him, it seemed, when she was little. He fell away from the church when Hitler publically persecuted the church. Many, including Mother, emerged from the war with a more personal and profound relationship with their creator that blossomed. For others, any concept of God was forever shattered into a million pieces of sand blown beyond retrieval.

Gertie chose to believe in science over God. But unlike her contemporaries, she was drawn to close the gap on human differences, ideals of superiority and retribution rather than study the seemingly minuscule differences of color, eye shape, height and such. Her view was simplistic in theory yet complex in execution: there is no need to look beyond our human form to see that we all belong to the same party, club, and nation. For Gertie, all people merged to form one nation; the human nation.

26

MOVING BEYOND HURT

S ally faded in and out of consciousness as she lay in the intensive care unit of St. Luke's Medical Center. Machines and canisters lined the walls, and mechanical sucking sounds kept beat in the background. Tall poles and machines surrounded her in a menacing way. Bright lights flooded her eyes every time she tried to open them. She did not have the strength to fight against the drugs and the lights. She fell back to sleep.

She heard voices far off in the distance, some familiar and others she did not recognize. "I'm sorry George but we just don't know when, or if, she will wake up again. Her head took a terrible blow when the truck hit her car."

"I want permission to let our daughters visit her. If anything can bring her out of this, it will be the girls. She loves them so much."

"Let's try it. Why don't you bring them by after school tomorrow? If she does not respond well or they get too upset, they won't be able to stay."

"Thank you, doctor. Nurse, will you let the other nurses know so we don't have any trouble getting in here tomorrow?"

"Certainly, Mr. Hunt. We will be certain to pass that on."

Sally fell back to sleep and dreamt of a young girl playing in the sun. This girl seemed familiar, with a baby blue ribbon in her dark curly hair. She was chasing another little girl whose copper hair flew as she ran away. They were playing tag, and the dark-haired girl could never catch up with her friend. Eventually, she collapsed into the grass and stared up at the clouds.

"Mommy, my class made this card for you. See, everyone signed it. The front has a picture of a pretty rose, and on the back is a picture of our family. Here is you in the hospital bed, Daddy standing there, Janna beside Daddy and here, this one is me." Carrie, the tender one, had a hard time looking at her mother's racked body. Her eyes focused on the card, as she narrated the details for her unseeing mother.

"Honey, that's very nice. Let's set it over here so she can see it when she wakes up." George didn't expect that they would waltz in and Sally would open her eyes. But he was hopeful that, over time, their voices would bring her back from the place she retreated to when the truck ran the red light and plowed through the car. A senseless accident that pushed his beautiful bride across the border to another land; a land with no language and no touch. A land he could not travel to.

"Momma, can you please come home pretty soon?" Janna leaned in closer to Sally's ear and whispered. "He only knows how to make scrambled eggs and it's kind of boring. He won't let me cook so please; won't you wake up and come home? We miss you."

George and the girls continued to talk to one another and to Sally. A doctor came in and adjusted the intravenous line. "Let's try to reduce the pain medicine some and maybe she will start to wake up some more."

There was no response from Sally that day, or the next. On the third day of visiting, a Saturday, the girls arrived with their father and Rona, who flew in that morning.

Sally stirred. She no longer needed the breathing tube and

in a raspy whisper, asked for a drink of water. That first day she was awake for only a few minutes at a time. "This murderous pain is taking the breath from my very existence."

George winced at this description of the pain and the look on her face. He would do anything to take the pain from her. "Sal, please just rest. We'll be back tomorrow to visit again. Is there anything we can bring you?"

She was already asleep from the medication and did not respond.

By the end of that following week she was able to sit up in a chair for brief periods and started to eat soft foods. She had no recollection of the accident and a spotty memory for the time immediately prior to the accident.

While Rona was still there, Sally asked her mother about the vision of the little girls playing outside. Her mother wasn't certain but thought she may have had a friend with copper-colored hair that she played with in Berlin. Once they moved to America, that part of Sally's life was never talked about. This was an opportunity for Sally to test her memory and learn more about her childhood.

Recovery was a long process. Sally had a broken pelvis, right femur and shoulder in addition to the head injury. She stayed in the hospital for nearly three months before she was ready to go home. The school year was already over. Despite the Chicago chill receding and the promise of a warm summer approaching, Sally fell into a deep depression.

George was now a partner in the architecture firm. Along with caring for the girls and visiting Sally in the hospital through late nights and weekends, he had managed to maintain his workload. He recognized, however, that Sally was at a critical juncture and really needed an intervention that would breathe some life into her weary soul. They planned a trip to Sweden, where they would live on a sailboat and travel along the western coast for the summer. They had talked about taking this trip when they first discovered they were pregnant with Janna. The time was not right then, but now seemed perfect.

A small light lit in Sally's eye when George proposed it as part of her recovery. She longed to be by the water, but knew her strength was not enough to be an effective hand on deck. They enlisted friends who shared a love of adventure to join them and help with the boat and the children.

The airplane ride was grueling for Sally. She paced the aisles of the airplane and napped between walks. She was stiff getting up and down. The doctors had told her to expect residual pain as full healing would take up to a year. They gave her an ample supply of pain medication, but she was reluctant to take too many as they made her so sleepy.

The girls entertained themselves and each other during the trip between naps. They played cards and drew on new drawing pads.

George brought some trade magazines to read, but exhaustion took over and he slept much of the trip. The long months of being a single working parent had taken their toll. This trip would be as good for him as it was would be for Sally. She hoped the worried look would disappear from his handsome face after time in the fresh air and sunshine.

When they landed in Gothenburg, friends were there to meet them. The boat was stocked and ready for departure. Their friends had been there for a week already, getting everything in order. Sally asked for time to walk around the harbor and check out the shops. She found a couple of books, sketchpads and pencils for herself. She was hoping to become inspired on this journey.

THE THREE MONTHS in Sweden went by quickly. The girls were terrific deckhands and learned to cook some on their own. Most of their protein came from the sea; fresh produce and supplies came from stops at small ports. Sally, on an impulse, bought several books including a *Bible*, *A Short History of the Jewish People* and *The Miracle of Forgiveness*, which she threw into her luggage.

By the time the trip was over, Sally was stronger in body and in soul. The readings, writings and drawings over the months helped her come to peace with the accident and the changes it brought to her and her family. On a deeper level, she wasn't quite at the point of forgiveness for the loss of her brother, father and childhood innocence, but she was moving in the right direction.

She found herself writing one passage over and over again, embellishing each with sketches of flowers. *She is clothed with strength and dignity and she laughs without fear of the future* (Proverbs 31:25).

A new sense of power was invading Sally, one that renewed her spirit and gave her hope for a brighter future.

27

GERTIE–COMRADE IN REPARATIONS

Gertie's drive to fulfill her purpose and make a difference was all-consuming. Time was wasting. The world needed to change. She travelled to Lisbon and set herself up in an affordable hotel. Sênior Bevis Rodrigue lived in the area. His was one of the names on the list provided by Olivia and Alex. Sênior Rodrigue was an associate of the Prime Minister of Portugal during World War II and was instrumental in helping to maintain Portugal as a neutral country. His mother was from France. Sênior Rodrigue inherited and still owned large masses of land in the northern region of France. His father's family had been in Portugal for generations.

Sênior Rodrigue lived outside of the political limelight in as reclusive an existence as possible, while still remaining active in international business ventures. He maintained a presence where and when he wanted. His staff included an assistant by the name of Sébastien Longpré. Gertie stared at the paper with the telephone number Alex gave her. She rehearsed what she would say to this prospective investor.

"Sênior Rodrigue, I am Gertrude Hall, an associate of Alex and Olivia James. On their recommendation I would like to talk to you about my work." Gertie thought that sounded too mundane.

"This is Gertie Hall calling. I'm a friend of Alex and Olivia James. Your name came up around the campfire at an archeological dig in Ecuador we were all working on. Can we get together and talk about some important work I'm doing?" She scratched out that introduction and decided she would just let it flow when she reached him on the phone.

She poured herself a healthy glass of bourbon before dialing. Fortunately, Sébastien picked up the phone on the other end and was able to converse in French. Only as she was dialing did she consider that there might be a language problem. She was certainly not fluent in Portuguese.

"Mister Sébastien, sir, my name is Gertrude Hall."

"Oh, Miss Gertie. We have been expecting your call, dear. Olivia wrote and told us you will be calling and that you had some big stuff to talk to Sênior Rodrigue about. We want you to come over; perhaps tomorrow at the dinner hour, if you can. Sênior Rodrigue is obligated tonight, but tomorrow is good."

Arrangements were made for dinner the following evening. Sébastien explained that he would send a car to bring her to Sênior Rodrigue's estate. She was encouraged to pack a bag and plan to stay the night, as Sênior Rodrigue was known to work late into the night on projects that interested him. He would be traveling out of the country the following day so this would be her chance to 'wow' him, Sébastien said.

"Now that was easy." Gertie said to no one as she hung up the phone. After a few moments of gratitude for Alex and Olivia, she finished off the bourbon and headed for the hotel's lounge to get her bearings.

Gertie sought information from locals regarding Sênior Rodrigue, his estate, and anything she could learn about his social and business activities. She learned that he had a wide variety of visitors from many nations and backgrounds, although the visits were infrequent. He was sentimental and frequently visited the homeland of his mother. He was close to his extended family. He no longer publicly advocated any political position. His religious practices were private, as was his relationship status. There was speculation that he was a gay man, but nobody would confirm it. What she heard from everyone was that Sênior Rodrigue was a man of flawless integrity and good humor.

After spending the evening in the local cantina gathering what information she could about Sênior Rodrigue and the Lisbon area, she retired to her room, hopeful that the meeting the following evening would be as favorable as she felt it would be. She still had some money in the bank but needed to secure funding in order to have an income and, more importantly, make a difference.

In the morning Gertie set out to find appropriate attire. She found a professional, conservative, long heather-grey skirt and a slate blue turtleneck sweater. It seemed a bit warm for the area but was appropriately conservative, and most importantly, affordable. She also picked up a tan linen wrap dress as an alternative to change into if she was clearly ill-attired.

By the time the car came to take her to the estate, she had written and rehearsed a dozen business proposal speeches. Finally, she had one prepared that was heartfelt yet not sappy, informative yet not too technical, and exciting without being too rehearsed. The driver made her feel at ease. The drive was about three-quarters of an hour into the countryside northwest of Lisbon.

When she arrived at the estate, Gertie was greeted with warm hugs and broad smiles. The manor was a regal nineteenth century palatial villa on luscious expanses of green lawn. Sébastien gave her a tour of the house. The interior was decorated with a surprisingly modern flair featuring crystal, chrome, and color accents throughout. She was invited to return when they had more time to tour the grounds together. "Sênior Rodrigue will be so disappointed if you don't come back and see his horses and his riding arena. He just loves those ponies."

Sênior Rodrigue was waiting for them in the study when the tour was complete. Sébastien poured them each a drink, and they shared small talk. After a cocktail Gertie realized she just needed to let the evening unfold and share her vision freely. She knew Alex and Olivia wanted her to succeed and would not put her in a position where she would have to compromise her integrity to achieve that. As the evening progressed, she understood just why Senior Rodrigue had made the top-ten list.

Sênior Rodrigue shared some of his history, his view of the world and his aspirations. After the first bottle of wine, it was clear that he and Sébastien shared more than just a professional relationship. Gertie, who routinely defied social graces, inquired about their relationship and how long they had been together. They both blushed slightly before going on to explain how they had met. Sênior Rodrigue was maintaining the public front of being a straight man. Beautiful women for whom he displayed the usual affections often escorted him. Invariably there would be a breakup when Sênior Rodrigue showed no sexual attraction. It was during a business trip to Paris that Sênior Rodrigue met Sébastien. Sênior Rodrigue wanted to buy something special for one of these women. This woman, Francesca Marquez, was stunningly beautiful and utterly charming. She was the first of his women to discover Sênior Rodrigue's personal preference. She agreed to play along and keep his secret, knowing that one day she would meet Mr. Right. Until then, she was content to be treated well by a very kind gentleman.

"Sênior Rodrigue, what is it I can help you find today?" Sébastien had seen Sênior Rodrigue in the store previously, personally selecting gifts for family members. It was apparent that money was no object. Sébastien looked forward to making a large sale.

"Hmmm. Suddenly I'm speechless and cannot remember what brought me in." Sênior Rodrigue smiled at Sébastien.

"Perhaps you came to select something special for Miss Marquez?" Sébastien had seen headlines regarding the two of them in the social section of the news some months back when they traveled to Paris together.

"Ah, yes, you are a smart boy. Of course. I need one of those gifts to make everything all better. Something to make her forget any misstep I have ever taken with her. Do you have something like that?"

"Yes, we certainly do. If you please, I would like to show you this new collection of Wander Paris hinged diamond wrist cuffs."

"Sounds interesting. Yes, please, pick out your favorite and show me." After complimenting Sébastien on his exquisite taste, Sênior Rodrigue asked that the gift be wrapped and personally delivered to Sênior Rodrigue's suite. That was the beginning of their beautiful and lasting relationship. Sênior Rodrigue set up Francesca Marquez in a flat of her own, funded for a year. Free to socialize independently, she did meet her Mr. Right and enjoyed a happy life, remaining forever true to her promise to keep Sênior Rodrigue's private life private.

Gertie understood the attractions. Sébastien was youthful in appearance with a lean, defined build. He was tall with a full head of dark hair speckled with grey. His hands were elegant, with long fingers and manicured nails. His complexion was dark Mediterranean. Sênior Rodrigue was older, with a distinguished and more traditional appearance. His face was kind and easily lit with a smile. He was quick-witted with a keen sense of world affairs. While wealthy and well-bred, he was not pretentious in the least.

Sênior Rodrigue asked Gertie many questions about herself and her goals for the future. He was deeply struck by her desire to confront racial prejudice. He shared his ties to the

Jewish culture, including a grandmother who practiced the faith.

Late in the night, after Gertie shared the newfound knowledge of her father's likely suicide and the failing health of her mother, Sênior Rodrigue took on a fatherly tone. He encouraged Gertie to embrace her roots and stop hating the fact that she was German. The Holocaust, he explained, was a pivotal life experience for her, as it was for non-Germans. He applauded her efforts to deconstruct the atrocious actions of misguided Germans and rebuild them into something far more positive and valuable. He agreed to support her efforts, up to $20 million over the following five years, on a dollar-for-dollar matching basis. He shared some ideas on how she could raise the matching funds and gave her names of others who may also be interested in supporting her work.

In the early morning hours, Sênior Rodrigue and Sébastien excused themselves and retired, arm in arm, for the night. Gertie was invited to stay on until later the following day, when a car would take her back into Lisbon. Gertie spent the next several hours seated in the window of the study, gazing at the stars and reflecting on the night's conversation. What a blessing it was to meet people of such incredible integrity and vision. She tearfully lamented the years she allowed herself to be consumed by hate and disdain for her father's political activities and her mother's acquiescence.

With the additional insights from Sênior Rodrigue, she examined her own approach to the world and relationships. She sobbed deeply, releasing emotions held tight in her core, much of which she could not label. As the sun rose, she slid between the crisp, cool sheets, grateful for newfound friends and business partners, old friends and lovers, Olivia and Alex, and the life experiences that inspired her vision and drive.

28

THE RESURRECTION OF ANATOLE

After nearly two decades of serving as Sister Marie's assistant, Sister Anna had become well versed in healing with homeopathy and botany. Sister Marie was aging and in her advanced years developed crippling arthritis, which neither of them was able to heal completely. They made methodical adjustments to her diet and applied poultices. They tried every combination they could think of to provide relief to Sister Marie's aching joints. They were successful for a time, but no remedy lasted.

Sister Anna revisited the notes she had maintained during her assistantship for clues. She periodically assessed Sister Marie's attitude and always found her to be positive.

"Sister Marie, do you have any worries or cares that I can assist with?" Sister Anna would inquire, hoping to break the grip that the arthritis had on Sister Marie.

"No Sister Anna, I do not. I am learning the art of patience." With that, Sister Marie would stop the conversation.

One night, when Sister Marie's pain was overpowering, she urged Sister Anna to go out on a house call on her own. A young boy had fallen from a tree. The doctors had treated him at the hospital for broken bones, but he had not fully regained consciousness. After observing him and attempting many medical strategies to encourage him to wake up, the doctors sent him home to continue healing. They would not predict his ultimate fate.

The family discovered, while still at the hospital, that if they put a cup or spoon to his mouth, he swallowed, but he would not open his eyes or speak. This continued on for three weeks. The family was not active in any church, but were neighbors of a parish family who asked on their behalf for Sister Marie to see them. Previously helped by Sister Marie with one of their ill loved ones, the family thought she could assist where the physicians had run out of ideas. Sister Marie refused no one in need simply because they practiced a different faith and was particularly inspired to assist when the patient was of no faith. Now it was Sister Anna's turn.

Sister Anna gathered a wide assortment of plants and packed a mortar and pestle. She arrived at the family's home on a Saturday morning. The boy's papa was outside working with the other two sons. The mama, Blanch, was in the kitchen with a crying baby on her hip, stirring something on the stove. She looked exhausted. Sister Anna explained that Sister Marie could not tend to their son, but she had studied with her for a long time and was there in Sister Marie's stead. Blanch introduced Sister Anna to the injured son, Anatole, who lay motionless on the bed except for the regular rise and fall of his chest.

Sensing that Anatole was stable and his mama racked with fear and fatigue, Sister Anna first talked Blanch into taking some fluids and a rest. The baby was young enough to still be nursing. She asked Blanch if the baby was fussy often. With tears streaming down her face, the exhausted woman indicated that the baby, a girl, had become fussy in the past two weeks and could not be calmed.

Sister Anna brewed some fenugreek tea and encouraged Blanch to have some water and the tea before she lay down to rest. While working in the kitchen, Anna looked out toward

Blanch's husband and other sons, who both appeared to be slightly older than Anatole. They were hardworking, maintaining the farm to keep the family fed and have surplus to sell to fund essentials they had to purchase. The equipment was old but appeared to be operational. Hannah surmised that this same farm had been in the family for many generations. The boys' father shouted orders to them to feed the animals after they put the field tools away.

After swaddling the baby girl, Hannah prepared a bottle of weak lemon balm tea. The baby took it eagerly before falling asleep. With the mama resting after water and fenugreek to stimulate milk supply and the baby sleeping after drinking the calming lemon balm, Sister Anna turned her attention to Anatole.

Anatole was a beautiful child. Dark wavy hair stood out from his perfect face. There were no bruises or cuts on his face. His lips were red and dry. His left arm and leg were bandaged. There was a splint on his leg to keep the bones straight while they healed back together. Sister Anna set out a small ceramic bowl and placed in it a small piece of Frankincense resin. She lit it and let the scent drift through the small home. The Frankincense would bring much-needed calm into the home. From years of experience, including her own experiences as a child, she understood the even when unresponsive one can smell and hear.

While working, she hummed her favorite hymns. She wanted Anatole to know that she was there with him, even if he couldn't see her. She blended some castor oil with ground ginger root, arnica montana, dried wild rose hips and sage. Touch, she believed, was very important in the healing process. She massaged Anatole, turning him side to side to relieve the pressure on his back. She spoke to him, telling him what his family was doing and describing the things in the room familiar to him.

After the long massage, Sister Anna returned to the kitchen

to prepare a special tea for Anatole. She sensed that he was there behind a shadow that he fell into when he tumbled out of the tree. The doctors had said there was no serious head injury, and they weren't certain why he could not be awakened.

From her supplies, she took the tins with rosemary, hyssop, gingko, cramp bark and arnica flowers and placed them on the counter. With these ingredients she steeped a tea, strained it and added a touch of honey. She also pulled out a jar of ham and bean soup that Sister Clara, one of the incredible cooks from the monastery, had sent. Whenever they visited a home Sister Marie and Sister Anna took something nourishing from the monastery's kitchen with them, both for themselves and for the families they were tending to. Quality nourishing food was not always at the top of the priority list when families were managing a health crisis in the home. The monastery's food was filled with love and nutrition and was a blessing to those families who received it.

Sister Anna returned to Anatole's room and set the tea down to cool while she gathered pillows and cushions from around the house to support him while sitting upright. Sitting up would help with blood flow and muscles. It would remind him what was normal for his body to do before the accident. Eventually, when someone was available to help, she would get him into a chair to sit for a while.

Once situated, she gave him the tea. Anatole sensed when the cup was against his lips and sipped. There must have been enough honey to make it palatable as he drank the entire cup over the next half hour.

Sister Anna returned to the kitchen to pour another cup. The sun was approaching the horizon, and dinnertime was near. The baby stirred, rooting around for her next meal. Blanch woke when she heard the baby moving, with a new sparkle in her eyes and full breasts ready to give nourishment to the baby. Blanch's husband Andre and their other three sons came in from outside. They had completed a full day's work and brought fresh milk in. After introductions, the boys set the table for dinner while Blanch and Andre visited Anatole for a few minutes. The family sat down to dinner and invited Sister Anna to join them. They enjoyed the soup and fresh bread. Gratitude filled the air.

After dinner, Blanch picked up the dishes and Sister Anna returned to Anatole's room with his brothers. Andre rocked the baby, who was no longer fussing. The boys took turns reading to Anatole or telling him about their day and how much they missed playing with him. They each kissed him and settled in for the night in their rooms. After the children had gone to bed, Blanch and Andre returned to Anatole's room where Sister Anna was again applying the massage oil. As they watched, she explained the formulas for the tea and the massage oil and shared her hope that in time Anatole would return to them. Sister Anna sat by Anatole's bed as the family slept, nodding off between singing and silently praying.

The following day was much the same as the first with the family going about their chores. Blanch rested again and the baby, Sophia, was much more pleasant. She smiled and played with her hands, watching as her mama worked around the house. Blanch helped with Anatole's first massage and learned how to fix the tea. Sister Anna and Blanch made a thick broth from boiled bones and grated potatoes, beets and carrots. Anatole drank everything they offered him. Blanch found a chair they could safely prop him in and a stool to rest his broken leg on. Anatole sat up for several hours that day.

"You know, Andre blames himself for Anatole's fall," Blanch quietly confessed to Sister Anna as they cooked together. "There is always so much work to do, and the boys know that they have to finish their chores before they can play. Andre was angry with Anatole for climbing in the tree instead of gathering the eggs that morning. Andre yelled at Anatole to get down from the tree and shortly after that he fell to the ground."

Anna nodded with understanding. Poor Anatole was scared to return for fear he may be in trouble. Anna knew what she had to do.

Two more days and nights passed, with Anatole taking in more and more tea and soup. Each batch of soup grew thicker with more ingredients. When she had the opportunity, Anna encouraged Andre to assist her with the massages.

"It is a unique opportunity we have to give our loved ones a healing touch. The healing is in the oils as much as it is in our touch that conveys what words alone cannot always relay. It is important that your heart is filled with all the love, acceptance and, where necessary, forgiveness, that you can muster."

"Thank you, Sister. I understand. Blanch and I are very grateful you are here. I will do Anatole's next massage if you don't mind." Andre's eagerness to heal his son delighted Anna.

The family developed a routine of feeding, massaging and reading to him. As fear and anxiety seemed to leave the home, Sister Anna changed the Frankincense scent to the lighter and sweeter scent of citrus alternating with rose oil on cloths in Anatole's room.

On the fourth day after her arrival, Anatole opened his eyes and was tracking the movements of people when they were in his room. He smiled at his siblings but had not yet uttered any sounds. The fourth night Andre asked to sleep by his side so that Sister Anna could get a full night's rest. She knew that she would have to leave soon to return to the monastery. The family seemed comfortable with their new routine, yet Sister Anna sensed something was about to change. She fell into a deep sleep on the family's sofa. During the night Sister Anna had another dream. She had experienced many since that first one with Sister Marie by her side when she first arrived at the monastery. With each one she gained knowledge that assisted her in her healing service. She was given the names of new plants to try and new applications for plants she already used. She was given foresight into situations that would occur.

On this night, Sister Anna was granted two important pieces of knowledge. Once again, the man who had presented her with the basket of flowers in the first dream approached. Again he handed her a basket. In the basket were familiar journals, those she had kept over the years to record botanicals and homeopathic remedies as well as information about patients and healing experiences. Lying on top of the journals was a sprig of thyme.

"Two young boys will come into your life. One is the boy you are with now. The thyme is for him. The second will come when you are near the end of your service on earth. Your notes will be critical to his studies in the healing arts."

Sister Anna awoke in the morning to a quiet house. She peeked into Anatole's room and found both he and his papa fast asleep. In the kitchen she set out to brew tea and make porridge for Anatole when his papa awakened. She did not want to disturb him. She presumed he had sat up with Anatole into the early hours of the morning.

She added thyme to Anatole's tea that morning, as Sister Anna recalled bits and pieces of her dream. She had developed an acceptance of these dreams, and while she did not blindly follow them, she heeded the information that came to her.

Within the hour, the house was alive with the family getting ready for the day. Sister Anna went to Anatole's room. She knew this may be her last day with him. She shared prayers of gratitude with Anatole and said the "Our Father" aloud. Anatole drank the tea without difficulty. As she was finishing, Andre came in with fresh massage oil that Blanch had made. They had taken such an interest in helping their son and mastered all the formulas and instructions Anna provided.

"Good morning, son. It's a new beautiful day. The sun is shining, the fruits are ripening and your mama's fresh laundry will dry on the line today. Little Sophia is getting her teeth already."

Andre started the massage. Sister Anna left the room to help Blanch with the breakfast dishes and the baby.

"Blanch, Sister Anna, come quick!"

Blanch put the baby down on the floor and ran to Anatole's room. Anna followed closely behind.

"Watch here." Andre picked up Anatole's arm without the bandage to massage it, and Anatole pulled it away. He had never before responded; his limbs always lay limp as his body was manipulated.

"Andre, put his hand on your face," Sister Anna advised.

Andre picked up Anatole's hand and leaned in closer, placing Anatole's hand on his own cheek. Anatole's fingers moved against Andre's cheek. Andre moved Anatole's hand to his nose, then his mouth. He kissed Anatole's fingers and spoke about how happy he was that he could feel him and how sorry he was for yelling at him to get down from the tree. Anatole turned his head toward Andre's voice, a tear visible in the corner of his eye. Sister Anna stepped out to pick up the baby and returned to Anatole's room with Sophia and the brothers. Blanch stood beside Andre, tears of joy rolling down her cheeks. Anatole had opened his eyes. A slight smile appeared on his face as he saw his brothers. Andre and Blanch then went through each of his body parts, asking Anatole if he had pain. He shook his head "no" until they reached his broken leg to which he quietly said, "A little."

"I love you, Papa. I promise, I will do my chores as soon as I am healed."

29

SALLY'S SUITCASES

I t was springtime. Sally was looking forward to the start of summer break when she would have more time to devote to camping and exploring with the children. She and George wanted their children to gain the same appreciation for nature and the outdoors they shared. They knew the pre-high school years were critical for nurturing respect and appreciation for the environment, so they set aside several weeks every summer and planned adventures in nature. This spring day was a day for planning, and the family gathered around the table to share their thoughts.

"I want to go back to Sweden." Janna, now in middle school, talked about that trip often. The Sweden trip had impressed her in ways Sally could never have imagined. She loved being on the boat, learning the names of the fish and the stars, observing the angle of the sun and the different types of vessels. She loved meeting new people; even topless sunbathers did not faze her. Janna kept a journal during that trip and would sometimes bring it out to share an observation she had made.

"Mom, can we go to New York and see Grandma?" Carrie

was their reserved homebody so they welcomed any suggestion at all from her.

"Yeah, maybe she wants to go camping with us!" Janna's enthusiasm was good to hear. A big trip like the trip to Sweden just was not an option this year.

Sally looked to George for his input. "Well, I was thinking this year I could take three weeks off and we could do a nice long trip to the coast. If your grandmother is okay with it, and I'm sure she will be, we could spend a few days with her. It would be a nice break from sleeping in the tent every night. We can invite her to camp with us but don't be disappointed if she can't join us, okay?"

Because George sometimes had to make business calls to different time zones outside of office hours, they had a new push-button phone with long distance service. Sally used it often to check on her mother. This was a good day for that. It was May first, and Sally knew her mother would think of Isaac. An invitation from the children to go camping may be a welcome distraction on this day, which she usually spent in isolation and prayer.

Sally's mother was delighted to hear from the children and excited with the prospect of a visit. She would consider the offer to go camping. She loved spending time with family and wished that she could live closer. However, the security of a familiar life and gratitude for a fulfilling job kept her in New York. She did not want to rock the boat. She made the trip to Chicago about every other year and wrote frequently between visits. Mail from Grandma was always welcome. The letters were full of her own stories, and parcels contained books with her illustrations.

After speaking with George on this May Day, she asked to talk to Sally. "Do you remember how I have written to the Jewish rescue groups about Isaac?"

"Yes, Mama, I remember. You have done it for years. Have you heard something?"

"Nothing about Isaac, I'm afraid. But I do have some news. In those letters, I also made inquiries about the people we stayed with and those who helped us get to America. I know you probably remember little about those times, but I have to tell you that when we left Berlin, I had packed some special, personal things from our house. We each had one bag when we packed up the car. We had to leave them behind at the first farmhouse we were at because there just was no room in the truck where we hid. Anyway, I'm sorry to bring all this up, especially on this day, but those suitcases... I can't believe it! That family saved those suitcases for all these years. I received a letter from one of the Jewish rescue groups. That family had contacted them to locate us. They wanted to return the suitcases and our things to us. Sally, it's been nearly 30 years, and they kept those things all this time!"

"Oh Mama! I can't believe it. Do you need to send some money? Can I help?"

"That's the greatest blessing. The Jewish rescue group agreed to bundle it up and ship it to me. Maybe by the time you come this summer it will be here. It doesn't bring back our Isaac, but it will be a gift to have some of those things returned to us."

Tears gently streamed down Sally's delicate face. With a puzzled look, George reached over to comfort her. He placed his hand on hers. "I love you, Mama. We'll talk again soon. We look forward to seeing you this summer."

PART IV

BEYOND BERLIN – LIFE PURPOSE

30

GERTIE'S MISSION

The moment Dr. Jurè opened the box she felt it; like a fist sprung from the container and slammed hard into her solar plexus, leaving her breathless with all the vitalizing air forced from her body. Without conscious thought, images of mass graves, lifeless corpses, children hidden in confined spaces, and mothers standing in the streets crying out for their children amongst the rubble of fallen buildings flashed through her mind.

"Dr. Hall… Dr. Hall, you look a bit peaked. Here, take this chair."

Gertie lowered herself onto the cool steel chair and dropped her head between her knees. She systematically assessed her body. *'Did I sleep last night? Six hours, that's good. Did I have breakfast? Cheese and bread. Am I pregnant? Definitely not. Do I have a fever? No.'*

"My apologies Dr. Jurè. Last night's festivities must have caught up with me. May I please have a drink of water?"

'Gertie, pull yourself together. You did not do this. You don't even know where he came from. This boy may have died right here in France after falling into the river while fishing, or having fallen down a flight of stairs. Deep breaths. That's right. Here he comes. Stand up. Take the water.'

Gertie moved around the table gazing at the several open boxes of bones until she found herself in front of one particular box marked "Male, Child, Berlin".

"Do you have any history on this body? Do you know why it is here?"

"From the notes maintained with the box, this boy was a German Jew who, along with several other subjects, was being studied before he died."

"Studied? Was he operated on?" That overwhelming feeling of dread started at her feet and moved up her calves. She steeled herself before her knees could buckle.

"Oh, no, nothing that barbaric, like some stories we have heard. These scientists were on the front-end of morphic measurements and anti-racial theories. The data they collected was entirely comprised of external physiologic dimensions. We do not know why the skeleton of the boy was maintained but there are many manuals of data, all drafted in German, that we have not examined. Oddly, they were, intentionally or not, actually disproving the Nazis' platform regarding racial superiority."

"Dr. Jurè, what are your plans with this boy and these materials? Must they be preserved as evidence of some sort?"

"That is why I contacted you, Dr. Hall. I am familiar with your studies on race, or non-races as you might say, and thought perhaps there may be something of interest to you here. Certainly you would have a better chance at understanding the journal entries than we non-Germans would. Are you interested?"

Gertie felt as if she had been handed a newborn child to nurture and grow into a being of substance. This was a gift beyond all others she had ever received. She turned away to pause for a moment, as if she had to consider the offer. While looking away, she wiped a tear of honor and joy that leaked from her eye. At nearly forty, she had shelved any thoughts of actual parenthood. Her work and now these precious remains were her surrogates to be looked after and mothered.

"Yes, Dr. Jurè, I will take possession of this boy and the other materials left here by the German scientists. I will maintain the collection intact so that if it is ever needed in the future as evidence, it will be available."

"How many boxes are there in total?"

"There are sixteen boxes. Each appears to contain one complete skeleton and has a notebook within it that is labeled just the same as the box. The labels show the gender, the general age, and the place of birth of the subject."

Gertie's heart raced and the little girl inside was jumping up and down with joy. She had become skilled at managing this duality of herself in professional life. It was in her personal life where she could not manage balance.

She had become accustomed to serially monogamous relationships. As soon as a partner commented on her habits and patterns, she immediately kicked them to the curb. Perhaps she needed therapy around the subject but then thought better of that idea and accepted herself for who she was: Gertie Hall, explorer of life, love and relationships of all magnitudes.

Gertie named the skeleton in the box labeled male, child, Berlin "Jacob" and saw to the careful packaging of Jacob and the others for shipment to her lab in Australia. With immense gratitude and the obligatory yet heartfelt kisses on the cheeks of Dr. Jurè and his colleagues, she and this wonderful new gift left the University.

31

HIDDEN GIFTS

T he remainder of the semester passed quickly, and summer arrived. The family started their summer camping adventure the first week in July. They explored the shores of Lake Michigan and fished for trout. They spent some time in a campground in central Ohio. George and Sally preferred to pitch the tent for a couple of nights at a time to avoid making the entire trip about setting up and taking down camp. Years ago they decided that a tent trailer or a camper would create an unnecessary barrier between them and the earth, and there were more opportunities to teach basic survival skills if their only shelter was a canvas tent. Air mattresses under the sleeping bags, however, were not out of the question; comfort also was important.

From Ohio they moved into Pennsylvania, a haven for campers. They drove north up to Lake Erie and stayed at a commercial campground. They met some wonderful people there, and the girls got to play with other children. During the day they explored by hiking the woods, crossing streams in the heavy forest on suspended log bridges or renting canoes to paddle the peaceful waters. They spent evenings sharing meals and swapping stories around the campfire with other campers.

They arrived in New York in the late afternoon on a Saturday. Sally's mother, Uncle Morris and his family welcomed them, camping grime and all. Rona lived in a large rent-controlled apartment building with parking about a block away. After several trips, they had the car unloaded. They draped the tent on the balcony to dry out. Campfire scent filled the apartment. They set the coolers to air out, and put the camping dishes in the sink to soak. Sally's family took turns taking warm baths and changing into fresh clothes as Rona started the laundry. By dinnertime they were refreshed and hungry.

Like Sally, Rona was thin and fit. She walked to work and to the market. She loved to cook and prepared a beautiful meal for them that night. Morris had chilled a beer for each of them. After dinner and putting the children down in makeshift beds on the floor, the adults sat and sipped on the cold beer. It was hot and muggy in New York; the windows and doors were open, and fans helped to move the air through the apartment.

Excited to share the things she had received from Berlin, Sally's mother asked Morris to bring out a series of four boxes. The Jewish rescue group determined the suitcases were too worn to travel and boxed the belongings to ship to New York. The boxes were delivered a couple of weeks prior but Sally's mother had not opened them. She wanted to share this moment with her family. She knew exactly what the boxes contained. Over the years she had reviewed those final days in their Berlin home when she carefully chose what would go in each bag.

In the first box they discovered Rona's father's prayer shawl. Rona had kept it in remembrance of her own father along with a photograph of her parents that was wrapped in the shawl. There was a hand-carved wooden box. "Your father gave me this box as an engagement gift."

One by one Sally's mother took several pieces of jewelry out of the box, tracing each with her fingers and examining them. She described each item and where it had come from. Some were now antiques from Sally's grandparents, and some were gifts from Sally's father. There were two sets of Shabbat candlesticks, a sketchbook and charcoal pencils, a hairbrush, and some linens. There was one pair of now-dated dress shoes that once fit her mother's delicate feet. Sally's mother smiled, a distant look in her eyes. "My dancing shoes."

When they finished examining this box, they settled into their seats and reminisced about Sally's father, his profound love of music, and tremendous passion for his family. Sally's uncle got them each another cold beer, and they opened another box.

One by one they went through all four boxes. The box dedicated to Sally's father Ira contained a yarmulke, a packet of currency cocooned within two record albums, a hand-written score, and a sweater that Sally's mother knit for him. Wrapped inside the sweater was the family's menorah. Tears brimmed Sally's eyes as the menorah was exposed. Once central to her childhood home and lessons with father, in this moment the menorah was the symbol of a life long gone. Sally excused herself to the powder room for a moment to gain some composure.

When she returned, they were ready to open the next box. In it they found a porcelain doll with handmade clothes, two children's picture books, two dresses, one sweater and a bundle of hair ribbons. Sandwiched between the books was a framed drawing. Sally studied the picture. It was a pencil drawing of Sally's bare skinned father lying in an embrace with her young mother, also bare skinned, both facing the artist. "Mama, I do not recall this picture. It is exquisite. Who is the artist?"

Sally handed it to her mother, who traced her husband's face through the glass. "I did." She spoke softly. "This was a gift I gave to your father early in our marriage, when I had already knitted him more sweaters than he could wear and wanted to give him something special. The night I gave this to him, he wrapped me tightly in his arms and sobbed. He was so moved by my display of affection for him. He shook his head and said, 'I had no idea, I just had no idea.'"

"What did he mean Mama?"

"He had no idea I saw him as such a passionate, beautiful man and, he did not understand just how much talent I had. He later described feeling sad that he had robbed me of a promising life as an artist and did not feel worthy of me. I told him he had lost his mind, and he had better find it because he was stuck with me!'"

Laughter filled the room. "I don't know that I had a promising life as a famous artist because I had never thought of pursuing one. All I wanted then was to be his wife and the mother of his children. It was a very happy time."

Uncle Morris and his wife excused themselves for the night, promising to take the early shift with the children in the morning if the rest wanted to sleep in. The final box contained Isaac's things. There was a children's book of stories, two changes of clothes, a pair of shoes, some coins wrapped in a cloth, a small metal airplane, a stuffed bear, and a story Isaac had written at school. The room fell silent as each contemplated the life left behind. Before they retired for the night, Sally's mother read a letter that lay in the bottom of the box. It explained what they had done to box up the belongings and included an inventory and explanation of the things that were not included. "The following is a list of things we found in the boxes that we could not transport for fear they would contaminate the other items: one small tin of candies that were melted into a mass of indistinguishable matter, one handkerchief and its contents appearing to be colored wax for drawing, and one small, half-drunk bottle of wine."

They laughed about the list of things detained and retired for the evening. When they were alone, George wondered aloud, "What do you suppose ever happened to that baby that was left behind? For all we know, that baby could have been the one to send these things to you."

"Wouldn't that be something?" Sally was tired and emotionally exhausted. She could not let herself walk through the mental gyrations and "what-if's" regarding that baby. For all they knew, it could have died or may have been reunited with its mother. Sally didn't even know if the baby was a boy or a girl.

SALLY AND FAMILY stayed on with Rona for three days before getting back to the camping trip. Each evening they sat and studied the boxes again. Sally's mother told and retold stories about each thing and what it represented. The children were enthralled with the stories, none of which they had heard before. Their mother was carried away from that experience at such a young age that most of her memories were deeply repressed. The menorah returned to Illinois with them, after traveling along the east coast. Sally felt a piece of her lost self had returned home.

32

THE CONCORD INSTITUTE

The enormous Sydney Harbour Bridge rose from the pink-hued waters, standing boldly against the early morning sky. The massive arched steel structure framed the brilliant flaming sun as it rose, illuminating the pink billowy clouds reflecting in the waters below. Two vessels silently slithered out of the harbor. From a distance a barge slowly approached, appearing first like a child's newspaper boat on the water. As it grew in size and approached the harbour, Gertie's anxiety swelled.

'Get this right, Gertie,' she ordered herself. The precious cargo aboard was critical scientific evidence to support her thesis: based on ninety-two biological markers, artistic and sexual expression, all humans spawned from the same seed. This was a rather crude way of saying that all humans are brothers and sisters on some level and the atrocities committed in the name of racial superiority were founded in unfortunate scientific miscalculations; or pure evil. It was not necessarily a new concept, but the meaning and acceptance of it could change the way all people, nations, and governments approached the world.

This shipment contained not only biological samples, but

sketchbooks, dolls and assorted items all relevant to augmenting the biological argument that Gertie's work stood for. The premise was that humans were more similar to one another across races and culture than they are different. Amongst the biological materials was the skeleton of a Jewish boy who was a research subject at a University laboratory in France. His skeleton was found years after the University was returned to French control by the Germans, in a storeroom amongst jars and vessels of preserved biologic samples.

"Careful there." Gertie shouted to the deckhands who shuffled the artifacts and supplies as if handling the day's catch from the ocean. "That is critical scientific evidence."

Gertie doubted the shouts of caution would have any impression on these brutes handling her precious cargo. Their scientific exploration was probably limited to what they did with their wives and girlfriends under the covers in the dark of night, blinded by alcohol. With a heavy sigh, she marched toward the ship. She directed each move as the deckhands loaded the boxes and trunks onto a truck to be transported to the Concord Institute of Australia.

Three hours and much handwringing later, Gertie hopped into the passenger's side of the truck to escort the treasures to the lab. A small, underpaid but highly over-qualified staff was assembled at the lab and ready to start processing the evidence.

The Concord Institute of Australia was Gertie's baby: her contribution to the world. She conceived it and labored to secure multi-national funding to grow and nurture it. Few anthropologists had ever created what she had. When it came to funding, disease researchers generally overshadowed the gifting receipts. However, her work inspired intrigue from humanity councils in thirty-six countries. The presentation she made to the International Union for Human Rights alone netted twenty-five million Australian dollars.

Late in the night, the team completed the logging of biologics and artifacts. Developing maternal instincts leaked out as she pled with them to go home, rest and refuel. Like Gertie, each for their own unique reasons had passion for the lab's contribution toward world peace, however small it may be.

Gertie sat alone with her treasures. The skeleton of the young boy was displayed on a cold steel table, ready for deep analysis when the team returned in the morning. She reflected on her heritage as the daughter of a political figure in Hitler's regime. She was haunted despite efforts to suppress it. Early in her career she thought often of changing her name to one less Germanic; but of course knew that would not change her biological composition and would be contrary to her efforts to harmonize all ethnicities, backgrounds, colors, and races.

She briefly looked at the notes that were packed with "Jacob." It appeared that the German scientists were measuring physiologic features such as finger and toe length, lip and eye size, and bone length and comparing the measurements across races and cultures for similar age groups. The subjects were referred to in the notes only by alphanumeric codes, a common practice in managing artifacts, but in her experience, not so common in treating people. She and the team would study the metrics in hope of furthering their own work.

She made a vow to the silent Jacob lying on the exam table. "I am making it my personal mission to find out who you are. Your family must be missing you. I will get you back to them young Jacob."

33

GEORGE AND SALLY'S ORGANIC LIFE

"How are things going George?"

George was grateful for this group of men, some of whom had been his friends for over twenty years now.

"Things are good. Sally is dealing with her mother's death and the grandkids keep her entertained. When school starts again in the fall, she'll get back into her routine."

George hated lying to his friends like this, but he didn't want to hang a dark cloud over this day of hiking and fishing. After an hour's drive, they arrived at the trailhead. The hike was just three miles to the lake where they would shore fish for trout.

George took in a deep breath of the morning air, filling his lungs with rejuvenating oxygen, free of the city's grime he had never become accustomed to.

"How are the house plans coming?"

"Terrific. The final plans have been approved and we will break ground in September."

George had kept himself distracted from Sally's melancholia by focusing his energies on their dream home. Sally had always been prone to sadness, but now she seemed especially lost. George also found great joy in spending time with their grandsons, particularly Christopher. Now a pre-teen, he showed a great aptitude for all things outdoors with great interest in plants and animals. This summer he went to a special camp to study with botanists and zoologists from the University. For a young boy, his knowledge of botany was astounding. He studied the Native Americans' use of wild plants for healing and kept a series of notebooks where he recorded locations of plants, sketched their leaves, stems and flowers and added narratives regarding uses and other related information.

George created as many opportunities as he could to get both boys into nature. "Boys, you've got to keep your boots on the ground and remember where your food comes from. God gave us only one earth. We've got to take care of her."

George and Sally took the boys out hiking as often as they could fit it into their schedules. One late autumn day they hiked the Starved Rock trail along the Illinois River and explored the waterfalls and shapely sandstone canyons along the trail. Michael, the more athletic of the boys, challenged himself physically at every turn. He wore a backpack weighted down with rocks to increase his effort. He climbed the rock walls and ran up and down the trail while the others took their time taking in the sights. Christopher stopped to collect fallen leaves and study the moss growing along the damp trail. Both boys stood in the spray of water coursing over the trail from the cliffs above.

George and Sally looked down at their grandsons from the Hennepin Canyon bridge. Sally caught a glimpse of Christopher as he crouched to examine something on the earth's floor, and a vision of her brother Isaac flashed in her mind. Several times during his life she had thought Christopher resembled her brother and wondered what Isaac would have been like at Christopher's age.

George was lost in thoughts of his own. Without the grandsons and the house project, George wondered how he would have coped with the constant sadness in the home. Sally was not naturally spontaneous, and in recent years she became less interested in traveling or socializing outside the family and was sullen. She saw a therapist for a while, trying to sort out her anxiety. She worried about everything. She drove their daughters crazy with her early morning and late night calls to check on the grandkids.

At first, George managed by staying late at work and taking on extra projects. That came with additional challenges. George and Sally's once-hot life of intimacy had chilled significantly. Late nights at the office, the handsome George often found himself in the company of ambitious, spirited and beautiful women eager for his extra tutelage, in or outside the office. Soon George determined he had to stop working the late nights. He was wholly committed to his marriage, and even if Sally wasn't amorous like she was in their younger days, he was not willing to abandon her for a quick fling. That's when he turned his attention to drafting plans for their dream house. He remained hopeful that they would return to the physical, close relationship they had once enjoyed. George had hopes of a new beginning with Sally in their new home.

34

GERTIE'S SPEECH

D ear Doctor Hall;
The United Nations extends a warm invitation for you to speak at our General Assembly meeting to be held March 20, 2002 in New York. We apologize for the relatively short notice. However, given the recent apparent terrorist attack that defiled the U.S. city of New York and the continuing global terror, the program committee feels an urgent calling to promote messages such as yours and that of the Concord Institute.

Before reading the entire letter, Gertie knew she had to go. She knew this platform for sharing her life's work was likely the last opportunity to make a global difference, if any could be had. She had become discouraged by the global leadership's inability to motivate the masses to eliminate divisive language and actions. She quickly called her assistant to make the arrangements, which included not only the UN presentation but a handful of community and university presentations as well. She then sat down to write her speech.

Thank you. Thank you for the warm welcome and thank you committee members for the invitation to speak today. Please, remain standing for a few moments if you would.

Let me start by giving you a warning. I am now over 70 years of age. I no longer even attempt to conform to social niceties, and today will be no exception. To be honest, I never was much good at minding my manners, and I'm not particularly well known for being nice. But I am effective. My message for you is urgent, raw and demanding. It is critical, and it is unfiltered and comes with a great deal of homework. Are you ready?

First off, let's get comfortable with one another. I will take many of you outside your comfort zone, which you will have to get used to if you want to fulfill the vision of a truly United Nations. Take a moment to shake the hand of a person next to you. Good, good. Now, I bet you could tell me some things about the person you shook hands with. You could tell me the color of their skin, the nature of their clothing, and whether they were man or woman. Raise your hand if I'm right. Ah good, this would not work if I was wrong. Thanks, now please have a seat.

So, you noticed that in just a few moments you were able to compartmentalize that person next to you in certain ways and label them by gender and color, at the very least. Believe it or not, you were not born with those filters that cause you to make those distinctions. Those filters were taught to you and for many of you, you've done a fine job of teaching your own children those same quick judgments of others. Your parents taught you from a very young age that you are a 'strong boy' or you are a 'beautiful little girl'.

You there in the front row with the red tie. Oh, did I forget to warn you that this was an interactive lecture? No apologies. Stand up, please. You are a beautiful person. And you there in the yellow dress, stand up. You are a strong person. What's wrong with women being strong and men being beautiful? Nothing. Absolutely nothing. Yet in many of your cultures, the filters segregate such characteristics and label them as good and bad. A beautiful man often has a negative connotation, just like a strong woman does. This process of building false divisions between race, gender, ethnicity and the like serves to break us down and apart as humans. It is an illusion and is founded in fear.

For most of my adult life I have lived in Australia. But the truth be known, I was born and raised during my early years in Germany. My father was one of Hitler's officers. I used to feel such shame when I said that. As a young child I had no idea what was happening to the lovely people of Germany, some who were my friends and neighbors. Growing up in Berlin after the war and the holocaust, however, I could no longer remain ignorant of the atrocities perpetrated in the name of racial or cultural superiority. I'm here to tell you, don't get too comfortable in your houses, mansions and palaces. If we don't act now, the world can change in an instant.

I have since been dedicated to reparations for the victims of the holocaust. Just as important, however, is my work at the Concord Institute that, in some ways, parallels your own United Nations. From your very own articles of purpose, I quote this powerful statement. "The Purposes of the United Nations are to be a centre for harmonizing the actions of nations in the attainment of these common ends", the common ends being to maintain international peace and security and the removal of threats to that peace. Human rights for all humans is central to your stated purpose.

The basic premise I have been building on for the past 50 years is this: we are all part of one race, the human race. That's it. Seems simple and easy, doesn't it? Now, I want you to think about this. Think of the person in your family that you are closest to. Everybody has one. Perhaps it is someone in your extended family. Would you bring harm to them? Would you wage war on them? I'm going to venture a guess here that the answer would be a resounding no.

What if I tell you this? On a cellular level, including the RNA and DNA, the most miniscule but critical elements that make you who you are, the differences from person to person are negligible. In fact, research is now showing that individuals from one population may be more similar to people from another population than the one they were born into. Isn't that amazing? You may be more similar on a cellular level to someone on the opposite side of the world than your own parent, sibling, or even that person that you previously reflected on that you would never, not in a million years, wage war on.

So what are we doing people? I ask you again. What are we doing that we are willing to kill humans that are just like us and pretend that it's because they are somehow inferior? They ARE us. We ARE the same. There is only ONE, not US and THEM.

Please hear me again. WE ARE ONE. Racism is not part of human nature. It is taught. That is foundational to fixing the problem. RACISM IS TAUGHT.

So what can you do? STOP TEACHING IT! Stop putting a box on your government forms to signify race. Stop waging war against your brothers and sisters in the name of racial superiority. By the way, it's not just race but I include here anything divisive like religion and culture. Stop the gender biases. Look within your own houses and clean them up! This sort of discrimination, which occurs around the globe, is not accidental. It was designed to divide and conquer. To destroy. To control. It's a falsity!

Many brilliant minds have shared this message long before me. Right here in this country, Martin Luther King, Jr. said it when he said, "Darkness cannot drive out darkness: only light can do that. Hate cannot drive out hate: only love can do that."

STOP HATING. START LOVING! Look to your native peoples who have many teachings regarding the impact your actions today have on all aspects of the world for the next generations to come. Do you want to keep breeding hatred? Band together. Be the human race you are and save this world before you destroy it. Say you're sorry. Make a plan to do better. Practice tolerance.

There was an amazing woman that I had the privilege of knowing and learning from. Many of you have heard of her, and I think her work is particularly poignant now. Elisabeth Kübler-Ross was a psychiatrist from Switzerland whose professional work was taking care of the dying. You know, when you've lived your life and you're marching on towards death, many truths get told. She captured those truths and those observations, and in her very important work she gave the world some profound insights. One point of interest I will share is her symbolic butterfly. In publications she used the butterfly to symbolize the transformation that occurs with death. She adopted that from hundreds of images etched into the walls of the children's barracks of the Polish death camp, Majdanek, during her work at the end of World War II. Elisabeth said, "I believe that we are solely responsible for our choices, and we have to accept the consequences of every deed, word, and thought throughout our lifetime."

This comes after hearing what must have been thousands of confes-

sions from the deathbeds of her patients. Confessions of wrongdoing or more importantly perhaps, deeds and words not carried out. Love not expressed or acted upon. Those lost moments when the patient had been too busy or too distracted to reach out and share love with a fellow human. To you today, I say, reach out. Put down the sword. Unburden yourself from your self-consciousness and be the love in the world.

There is just one more point I want to make and actually, it is again from Elisabeth and can be found in many other writings as well. When we boil it all down, we have only two emotions: love and fear. Imagine your life if the fear were removed; if nations did not fear the power of other nations; if the entire human race lived harmoniously as one. What a powerfully peaceful world we would have.

Be courageous. Be intentional. Live while you are alive and give others something to talk about when you are gone. Allow your children and grandchildren to be the innocent, loving humans they were born to be. Mind your words. Bring love into your life. Examine your fears and dismiss them.

Finally, please join me on your feet again. These 70-something legs of mine are getting tired, but I have this one last challenge for you. In all of what I've said today, I have asked you to take a new path. To swim upstream to where you started as a loving human free of the falsities that have been imposed on you. Everyone in this room shares far more similarities with you than differences. This time, when I ask you to turn to your neighbor, I want you not to look at them with your discerning eye, but with your heart. I want you to look them deeply in the eye, reaching for their essence and their soul and seek the similarities. Ok, now. Don't be shy. Look directly. Look deeply. Seek to understand and accept.

In this moment, you are meeting for the first time your kin in the human race, linked in love and shed of fear. Feel this moment and take it with you. You are powerful. You can be human beings, not human doings, making the change in the world that is so needed and so critical to save the generations to come. It's not too late. There is hope.

Thank you all for your time and attention today.

Gertie put the pen down. She would refine the speech as the time came closer to present it. The urgency of the issues kept her up at night, resulting in exhaustion and irritability with her staff. Writing this speech was a reminder to use this message daily as she presented it to the world.

CONCORD INSTITUTE AT A CROSSROADS

"I simply cannot agree to fund a study whose thesis is to attribute terrorism to certain races or cultures. This kind of study, and it appears there are many of them seeking funding today, will not answer the fundamental questions this institute was founded on."

"Ms. Hall, with all due respect, in order to remain competitive in our future funding efforts for the Institute I feel strongly that we need to support those nations currently embroiled in efforts to fight terrorism." Roger Bankston was a board member that Gertie herself recruited to serve on the philanthropy committee of the Institute, but it had become clear over time that he had political aspirations of his own that he wanted to advance through his work with the Institute.

Exhausted after a grueling marketing tour for the Institute and anxious about the laboratory results she received the prior week, Gertie's fuse was short and she was irritated. In a poorly disguised condescending manner, she failed in her attempted jesting delivery.

"Mr. Bankston, I believe this board could agree to fund the study of the misapplication of philanthropic efforts by board members to win friends and influence voters, which many countries would be equally interested in studying; however, that will not happen on my watch and I will not, while I am still living and able to be a contributing member of this Institute, agree to fund any studies on terrorism. Now, are there any proposals that have nothing to do with terrorism and are actually aligned with the mission of this Institute? If not, I move that we adjourn this meeting so I can get on with something more productive."

After two hours of uninspiring proposal reviews, the board adjourned. Gertie retired to her office. She sat at her desk, overrun with files, mail and magazines. She rearranged the stacks of paper, clearing a place to lay paper and pen, and paused to clear her thoughts.

Although technically retired, Gertie continued to publish and speak on behalf of the laboratory-turned Institute that she founded. For four decades she had exhausted herself trying to repair relations following the Holocaust and bring scientific evidence to the forefront in an effort to quell the impassioned arguments of racial and cultural superiority. The 9/11 terror attacks on the twin towers had brought a new sense of urgency to the Institute's work. The impact made worldwide to that point was incremental and minute, but the momentum was building. Her once-modest laboratory had evolved into a full-blown Institute with international recognition.

Driven by feelings of guilt, injustice and horror, Gertie's journey had been to right the wrongs of people like her father. She was reconciled to the fact that he was a German soldier who deceived German-Jewish men in higher social circles in Berlin and placed their families at risk; all to further the efforts of Hitler whose mission was to eradicate peoples he believed to be lesser. Gertie was an unwitting accomplice when she invited her best childhood friends, Hannah and Sarah, to that May Day celebration those many years ago in Berlin.

Gertie took a deep breath in an attempt to quiet the anxiety rising in her belly. With arthritic hands she picked up and opened the ragged folder where she had compiled the last of the evidence for this final report. She placed the pen to paper and began to write.

"Dear Sally:

I am Gertrude Hall. I am an anthropologist living in Australia. You may remember me from many years ago as a neighborhood girl who lived near your family at Westarp 26, Berlin. You and I were once schoolmates and playmates. You called me Gertie. We shared adventures and told each other stories of growing up and exploring the world. We once enjoyed tea parties but outgrew them for the much more sophisticated games of tag and dreams of going to college. Your father and his ensemble played in our parlor many times, and you and I drew pictures of beautiful women dancing.

What I am writing to you today is long and painful. May I suggest you pour yourself a cup of tea and get comfortable as I lay out for you some very interesting, maybe even shocking, information? I pray your heart is well and can handle what I am about to disclose to you.

I have enclosed a photograph of myself, as well as you, your brother Isaac and our friend Hannah at the Maypole dance. I am the sassy girl with the big collared dress in the foreground. I recognize you as the girl with dark curly hair and your brother stands next to you, just a few inches taller. Hannah is above me with the bow in her hair. This photograph was part of the propaganda published in a Berlin newspaper intended to show how normal life in Berlin was and how happy the superior German race was. I have kept this photo and provide a copy for you now. You will soon see how this photo had been critical to me over the years.

I did not see you, Isaac, Hannah or your families after the police raid that day. Much later, I learned that my father and others of high rank in Hitler's army had tricked German-Jews into being at the May Day cele-bration that day so the soldiers could capture the Jewish families. I cannot tell you the betrayal and horror I felt at learning of this inconceivable action by my father. My parents have long since gone to their graves and have had to face their actions with a force much greater than I.

Lost in thought, Gertie did not hear the telephone ring or her assistant come to the door to say goodnight. "I'm leaving for the day Ms. Gertie. Mr. Matthew called. He asked that I remind you about your dinner date tonight."

"Oh my, what time is it? It's our anniversary dinner tonight."

"Yes, Ms. Gertie, you have been together ten years now. Maybe tonight's the night he will pop the question."

"Oh dear, he gave up that notion years ago. A man can only take so much rejection, you know. He just sticks around so he has a dance partner. Thank you and have a pleasant evening Ellie."

"Thank you, I plan to. Your dress for dinner is in the powder room. Your shoes and wrap are in the closet. Have a great time."

After years of being complacently single, hopping from relationship to relationship, Gertie met Matthew at a civic function. At the time her sixties were waiting in the wings and she had become bored keeping up with younger suitors. She was never at a loss for affection from a student, mentee or advocate. She had come to realize, however, that these younger men could not reminisce about the good old days, freely discuss sagging skin and sluggish bowels that come with aging, or how to manage an estate. Matthew came into her life at the perfect time.

She and Matthew loved to dance. For their celebration of ten years living together, they were going to dinner and then dancing. She looked forward to spending the evening gliding across the dance floor with a smile on her face held in the arms of handsome Matthew. Tomorrow she would finish the letter to Sarah, now Sally, and start planning for a reunion with old friends.

36
───────

SALLY'S LETTER ARRIVES

S ally shifted in the chair, laid the letter in her lap and took a sip of tea. A knot formed in her stomach as she read of Mr. Hall's betrayal. Sally had never before considered that her family was tricked or betrayed. More importantly, she sensed the angst her friend Gertie must have felt when learning of this. Sally spent her whole life either forgetting or forgiving the horrible things that happened in her childhood. It seemed Gertie had never let go and relived those horrendous days over and over again. Sally's heart ached for her childhood friend. She picked up the letter and continued.

"In the years since the war, I have made it my life's work to do two things: 1) advance world peace by dissolving ill-conceived notions of racial superiority; and 2) support reparations efforts related to the Holocaust. More importantly, and at the root of all I do, is my deepest desire to make up for the wrongs of my father.

I founded a center in Australia now known as the Concord Institute. There is no reason for you to have heard of it."

Sally put down the letter and stood from the comfy chair in

the library nook off the bedroom. She walked to her writing desk and pulled out a stack of papers clipped together. Leafing through the papers, she found an article written by Gertrude Hall. The author's biography described Gertrude Hall as an anthropologist, a philanthropist, and founder of the Concord Institute in Australia.

Sally's heart skipped a beat as she realized the synchronicity of everything. Returning to the chair, she took another sip of tea and settled back to continue reading.

"The Institute started as a laboratory to support my work in cultural unification. You see Sally, what happened to the German-Jews, and to many people of certain cultures over the lifetime of human existence, is against nature in my opinion. I have partnered with top scientists across the world to study the biology of humans, arts, sexuality, and culture in an effort to prove that we are all more alike than we are different. That each person has unique characteristics to be honored and the ideological theories upon which genocidal activities are founded are flawed. Races and cultures are not evil; individuals may be.

Now you know my soapbox and I must get back to the reason for my writing. In the 1960s, when I was a very young scientist, I acquired artifacts of captured and exiled German-Jews who had been transported to a laboratory in France for medical study and observations. Among those things were the remains of a young boy. Please take a deep breath. Sally, with the advances in scientific technology now, we are able to track DNA to family members across the world. I had that boy's DNA tested and compared to an international database of DNA."

Sally's heart skipped a beat. She recalled the day when her daughter Janna asked her to complete some papers and swab her mouth for DNA to be part of some Jewish-American database. Sally had shared the story of the war and her family with the children as they became old enough to understand it and she could share it factually, without overwhelming grief. Janna was herself a scientist, studying cancers and developing treatments. She became aware of this DNA database that was established to assist with reparations efforts, to trace families of Jewish affiliation who were displaced. Janna suggested that we might locate relatives.

"DNA of Isaac Fischel came up as a sibling match to Sally Hunt aka Sally Fischer. I know a lot of those exiled from Germany in the late 30s and 40s changed their names and I assume Fischer was once Fischel. Now that ship manifests are published, I had my researchers track Sally Fischer to Sally and Rona Fischer who sailed from Denmark to Ellis Island in 1940. Sally, your brother died as a young boy in France under medical care. I have read the records of his care and treatment and I can assure you that he was studied, but he was not tortured in any way. His death was not brutal. He became ill, and they were unable to cure him."

TEARS OF SORROW and relief flowed from Sally's eyes. She reached for a tissue and melted into the chair. Deep sobs and gasps for air overtook her. Decades of wondering and worrying left her body with each exhale. Finally, she stood and slowly walked to the kitchen to heat up the tea. George was working in the shop. She thought about calling to him, to seek comfort from him, but knew that what she felt needed to flow out and be released without interference. No amount of comforting words or touches from George could soothe the rawness exposed by this letter. The efforts of her mother to protect her by giving her a new identity had been violated by modern technology. The same technology solved the mystery of her brother's demise and would bring him back to her for closure. Exposed and vulnerable, Sally returned to the chair, lifted the letter in her delicate hands and braced herself for more.

"Sally, I would like to return Isaac to you and will bring him to you

wherever you designate, but there is more for you to consider. I have never married nor had children. Frankly, if I had a therapist, they would tell you my guilt and anxiety related to events in my childhood made me feel unworthy of happiness and unavailable for partnership. That doesn't mean, however, I have not had fun and meaningful life experiences.

Several years ago I enjoyed a beautiful friendship with a man whose family was from the northern region of France. He invited me to travel to his family's estate there. We toured the countryside. On that tour we visited a monastery with the most beautiful garden. We stayed nearby at a bed-and-breakfast and toured the grounds of the monastery over two days. On the second day of our visit we were invited to join the nuns for lunch. A group of sisters joined our table while we were being served. As we exchanged introductions, I sensed something familiar about Sister Anna.

Sally, I could not believe it. Anna was from Berlin and had been shuffled to the monastery with the rising violence against Jews in Berlin. She too sensed a familiarity in me, and we compared our childhood stories. Unbelievably, we discovered that Sister Anna is our childhood friend Hannah! We have stayed in touch in the years since that fateful day at the monastery. Her health is failing now. She has never been outside of the area she lives in since she arrived there so many years ago and is not able to travel. I know she would love to become reacquainted with you, as would I. I do not know your health status. If remotely possible, would you consider meeting in France, where we could see Sister Anna? I am willing to assist with any expenses necessary, if you do consider this."

SALLY PULLED from the large envelope a laminated newsprint article with a photograph of a group of children. The May Day celebration. Sally studied the picture. She barely recognized herself, but the image of Isaac was unmistakable. This is the memory of Isaac she had hung on to, to avoid thinking of what may have happened to him. The photo validated her sense that Christopher resembled Isaac at the same age, which eased Sally's concern that she had forgotten much of her brother. She held the picture close to her heart. Sorrow for his loss and gratitude for the new knowledge coursed through her.

Sally stood to look out the window at the flower garden she and George had cultivated over the years. True to his promise, George designed and built a stunning grand home. Living within the massive beams and hardwoods, Sally was grounded. She toiled in the garden, bringing dormant plants to full bloom year after year, just as her mother had done back in Berlin. The cycle of the plants reaffirmed for Sally what she had come to know about life. There would be quiet, dark days and then light and warmth came, illuminating all the wonderful, beautiful things around.

It seemed today that this cycle kept looping in extremes. Gertie's confession of her father's betrayal and the reality of Isaac's death brought such deep feelings of loss. Yet the promise of laying Isaac to rest and meeting Hannah and Gertie again was exhilarating. George found Sally staring out the window at the garden. She turned to him and smiled as he approached. "George, we're going to France."

PART V

BEYOND BERLIN – THE FINAL ACT

37

THE HOTEL

George wrapped his arms around Sally, as he had so many times over the decades. He looked over her shoulder to the paper in her hands. A 1938 Berlin newspaper photograph of a May Day celebration had been laminated. The faces of the smiling children belie the state of affairs. With a marker, Sally had circled four faces. George recognized the dark, curly-haired girl as his beautiful wife. Their daughter Carrie looked just like her as a little girl. Sal's brother Isaac, without the curls but with dark hair and eyes, stood just beyond her as they played the Maypole dance game. His face, so similar to that of their grandson, Christopher, as a young boy, was circled as well. Two others' faces were circled and the meeting with these two girls, now women, was about to take place. This day has been a long time in coming.

"Tell me again, Sal, about that time you almost met Gertie Hall."

"A couple of years ago I was tutoring a student, Martin Schmidt, who wrote an essay for his final paper in an English class. He had immigrated late in his youth and struggled with the English language. He made great progress, and his final paper was quite a masterpiece. He wrote about the scientific inaccuracies contributing to racial genocide, or something along those lines. In his paper there was a footnote that caught my eye. He cited a reference to a paper authored by an anthropologist out of Australia by the name of G. Hall. I researched the article and the author some and found out that G. Hall was Gertrude Hall and she was scheduled to speak at the University of Chicago as part of the Holocaust Reparations, but the events were cancelled due to 9/11. I thought it was a long shot that it would be the same Gertie Hall I knew, so I didn't pursue it any further. I did find her articles interesting, however. She was trying to extinguish the gaps between races through scientific theory to show, essentially, we are all the same and the Holocaust and other similar events across the world should never happen because it's like murdering your sisters and brothers."

Janna, their eldest daughter, walked into the hotel room just then, with her husband and two boys in tow.

"Mom, did you ever in your wildest imagination think that there would be a day when you would be reunited with your childhood friends from Berlin and finally have closure on what happened to your brother?"

"One thing I have learned for certain is that you cannot predict anything. If you had asked me when I was a little girl if Hannah would become a Catholic nun, I would have laughed in your face and run off to play. If you had asked me, when I first arrived in the United States, if I would find happiness and overcome my past, I would have said 'yes' because that is what was expected of me. But I would never have believed it, deep down in my soul. The beautiful life I have enjoyed, with your father, you girls and your families, my career, my mother when she was alive... all of it was not even a glimmer of hope within me before I met your father. At most, I had hoped to be an honest, hard-working, productive citizen. I am truly blessed!"

38

THE REUNION

S ister Anna eased into her seventies with grace and peace—fruits of decades of clean living, a low stress lifestyle in a community of like-minded people, and gratitude for the opportunity to fulfill her purpose on a daily basis. Parishioners and area residents continued to consult with her on their health, husbandry and gardening concerns. She had now published three handbooks on botanicals and homeopathic remedies. She was frail and moved about slowly; the soft, kind face and quick smile belied the constant pain in her knees and back from years of toiling, kneeling and bending over to nurture the plants.

Sister Anna, kind by nature, knew no strangers and was never cross. While she felt a peaceful love for all around her, she had never experienced deep personal love. She could not recall a time when her heart felt as if it would leap from her chest because she felt so close or attracted to another person. She heard tell of women, and men, feeling stomach butterflies when they were near someone they were drawn to, but never experienced that feeling herself. Her lifestyle did not lend itself to romance. She was grateful for the grace she was shown when she was saved as a young girl, but nonetheless curious about how romance would feel.

The monastery kitchen was abuzz with activity, much as it was those many years ago when she first met Sênior Rodrigue. A lifetime of memories played through Anna's mind. This day, the reunion with her childhood friends, was a gift she could never have anticipated. When Gertie wrote to her to share the discovery of Isaac's remains and the ability with new technology to locate Sarah, Anna was overwhelmed with emotion she had not experienced in years.

Reflecting on those early, carefree days in Berlin, she found herself smiling, inside and out. That happiness gave way to memories of her journey to the monastery and the loss of her family en route. Anna revisited some of her journals and the accounts she had written of babies delivered, comfort provided at death and emergency care given to accident victims. She had delivered nearly two hundred babies and tended to several hundred people and animals over the years as a lay midwife. She valued each day she was given.

In her work Anna met many people who were downtrodden, uncertain of their purpose and seemingly unable to find happiness in their lives. For those people she prayed the hardest, for she knew it was by the grace of God that she had been brought to her destiny. Looking back at her life's work, she knew there was no way she could have orchestrated her delivery to a loving community, a gifted mentor and the opportunity to learn and give of her time and talents in the ways she was able to. There was only one area in which she was unfulfilled and felt her purpose had not been fully satisfied. There was no longer a need for a midwife, so she had no student to follow in her footsteps as one. Yet she had not lost sight of the vision she once had while caring for the young Anatole who grew to be a handsome man with a family of his own. In that vision she was told that she would meet a boy with whom she would share the notes she had taken of the symptoms of her patients and the botanicals she used. She had not been in a rush to meet this boy because she knew it was to come toward the end of her days. Now, she was ready.

Anna toured the monastery and observed the preparations for the reunion that was to take place later that day. Her heart was warmed by the love with which the Sisters worked on preparations. The cooks prepared the food from fresh produce and homegrown meats. Fresh flowers were placed throughout the rooms and the table settings were stunning. The windows and floors were recently washed and quarters were aired out for the guests to spend the night if they chose.

Gertie and Matthew arrived in the early afternoon. Gertie felt a certain level of responsibility for the reunion and wanted to be on hand to assist, if she could, in the preparations.

Gertie and Matthew joined hands as they walked to the entry of the monastery. Matthew, Gertie's faithful supporter and sounding board, was as excited as she was for this reunion. Gertie was dressed in an expensive yet simple pantsuit that silhouetted her lean, tall body. Matthew was the handsome escort in fresh jeans and suit jacket. Anna and several of the Sisters greeted them at the door, essentially creating a welcoming line filled with joyful hugs. Anna's warm smile melted the hearts of Gertie and Matthew. Gertie and Anna quickly fell into a familiar pace. They caught up with one another while they worked on the final touches before Sally and her family arrived.

Matthew and Gertie unpacked and distributed the gifts they brought from Australia for the Sisters. There were tins of loose teas, jars of lanoline creams, chocolates, and cans of macadamia nuts. The Sisters delighted in opening the gifts, smelling the teas and creams and setting the nuts and chocolates aside to share later. Gertie and Matthew had stayed with old friends in the region and also brought local cheese and wine to share for the evening.

Anna sat with Gertie and Matthew, catching up and

sharing their excitement for the event about to unfold. Gertie and Sally had spoken on the telephone shortly after Sally received the letter. They made plans for retrieval of Isaac's remains for a proper burial and set the time and place for the reunion. Gertie was anxious during the call. Despite the many accomplishments in life, she felt words were inadequate to express how she felt about the opportunity to meet with Anna and Sally, to make amends on behalf of her father and the regime. Her lifetime goal of eliminating racial bias and educating the populace about the false pretense upon which ethnic and cultural wars are founded had not been fulfilled. She had, however, set a firm foundation in the anthropologic and biological arenas to continue the dialogue and education. The urgency of this reunion drove her for the past several weeks. She was prepared for what could be a very difficult conversation and fully anticipated being met with anger and judgment.

Sally and family arrived a couple of hours later. Sally waited for George to open the car door while the rest of the family piled out of their cars and gathered gifts and mementos into their arms to present to the Sisters. Sally was anxious. She did not have the strength to stand.

"Oh, why did I have to wear these silly shoes? That's what I get for being so vain."

Janna held out her mother's running shoes. "I think you will be more comfortable in these, and look, they match your pants."

The group laughed and a smile spread across Sally's face.

"I am so predictable, aren't I?" She changed her shoes and stood up from the car seat.

Sally feared being judged for the ways she had changed. She abandoned her Jewish faith, changed her name, and had never returned to Germany, even for a visit. The family paused while Sally gathered herself. When she was ready, she took the point position, walking to the oversized wood and iron gate leading into the grounds, with George following close behind in case she lost her balance. When she reached for the gate's handle, her hand shook so badly, she pulled it back. George wrapped his right arm around her shoulders and reached with his left to open the gate. As the family stepped inside the gate they were greeted by three Sisters, in habit and aprons, who excitedly approached them. The Sisters offered hugs and helped carry packages.

Sally's stomach danced with fear. She took in deep breaths as her feet cautiously advanced forward on the walkway. By the time they reached the door, Gertie and Anna were already waiting in the doorway. The emotional reunion that followed brought everyone to tears. Sally was first taken into the arms of Anna. They hugged, then held one another at arm's length, studied each other's face and looked deep into one another's eyes. Sally later described to her daughters how the decades of doubt about her changed identity, lost religion and uncertainty vanished. In that moment, she knew she was loved on earth and beyond by a God that was loving and kind. She was free of judgment of herself. Anna was pure goodness. She glowed with love and acceptance.

"Hey, it's my turn."

Sally turned to Gertie; they giggled at one another and embraced. Sally felt awkward with Gertie, who still seemed like a stranger. Although she hugged Sally warmly, Gertie did not feel the calmness she felt with Anna and hoped that by the end of the visit they would feel closer.

"And I'm George."

"Oh my goodness, how rude of me. This is my husband George." Sally introduced the rest of the family and Gertie introduced Matthew. Anna ushered them into the sitting room. They spent the next two hours sharing stories, memories and dreams. Anna shared her conversion to Catholicism and the training and practice as a midwife. She pointed out her journals where she recorded the conditions of patients, and the treatments attempted.

"Sister Anna, guests, it's time for dinner. Please join us in the dining hall."

"Oh, yes, Sister Grace, we will be right in. There is a toilet just there if you would like to bathe your hands before dinner." Sister Anna directed her guests to a hallway room.

Sally's family gravitated to her, surrounding and supporting as they transitioned to the dinning room. She assured them she was doing okay and encouraged them to enjoy their dinner.

When they had all assembled in the dining hall, Mother Superior Jeanne Louise said the blessing. "Blessed Redeemer, we give thanks for this evening of reunification, forging of friendships, and amends. By Your grace nations have come together despite great atrocities and human shortcomings. We truly honor and seek your glory. In your holy name, Amen."

The room filled with the clinking of toasts and forks on china accompanied by laughter and chatter. They dined late into the evening and finished with a lovely dessert and coffee.

Sister Anna invited all to spend the night, and all guests did so. As she showed them to their rooms, she took them to her first room in the monastery and described the disorientation and illness in the first few days there and the grace she was shown by the Sisters who came to her rescue.

As Anna spoke, Sally's heart swelled with the force of their Jewish roots and the resilience they had both shown in adapting to the new lives forced on them. Tears stung her eyes and streamed down her face as the stark reality hit her. Images of their early days together flashed in her mind. She reached out and grabbed Anna's hand as she led them out of the room.

"Oh, Anna. I just had no idea. You look so happy, so content, but obviously you had to surrender yourself to survive."

Anna turned to her and they looked deeply into one another's eyes. For a brief moment Anna's face showed uneasiness, then quickly recovered.

"And I am grateful every day that I had the opportunity to survive. So many did not. Any sacrifices I made in those early days have been rewarded a thousand-fold since."

In that moment, Anna felt the deep stirring she had never known: the closeness to another whose flesh she wanted to bond with. Later, as she sat in the library and reflected on this feeling, she determined it was not romance or lust that she felt, but a deeply rooted emotion unlike any she had ever known. A locked door opened deep within her, opening to a profound well of love and acceptance, of herself and others, on earth and beyond.

Before retiring to bed, Sally's grandson stopped off in the library to examine Anna's notebooks and publications. Sister Anna sat with him and explained her methods of observations and note taking. She encouraged him to look at the materials as long as he wanted, and if he had questions, she would be happy to visit with him after morning prayers the following day.

Christopher studied excerpts from various journals into the early hours of the next day. By morning he had a series of questions to pose to Anna. She enthusiastically described for him her observations, the influence of the state of mind on the patient, as she observed it, and her thoughts on raising healing plants. She relayed her first healing experience with a lame chicken and her tutelage under Sister Maria. Anna had not felt such enthusiasm about her work for years and was infused with memories she excitedly shared with Christopher.

Despite the late night, the entire party was up early the next morning, greeted by inviting scents from the kitchen and the sounds of dishes and cutlery. The dishes from the previous evening's party were cleaned up and a new feast prepared and ready on the table.

Over breakfast, the three friends exchanged gifts. Gertie

brought matching Australian opals for all the women and sheepskin toiletry bags for the guys. Sally had painted a picture of her mother's flower garden in Berlin and presented a framed copy to each of her friends. Sister Anna's gift stirred emotion in everyone in the room. It was simple and not expensive, but the story behind the gift took their breath away.

Anna rarely told the story of her escape from Berlin. She had not yet told her friends the entire story, and they had not pried. She handed Gertie and Sally each a box crafted from handmade paper. When they lifted the lids, each woman saw a beautiful purple ribbon shaped into a butterfly, its body adorned with pearls. Anna shared the story of the purple ribbon given to her by her father on that May Day when their lives changed forever. She described finding it freshly laundered and pressed, when she finally had the strength to dress after first arriving at the monastery. On that day she packed the ribbon safely away, preserving it to remind herself of the happy times with her family.

The group toured the gardens and walked along the fences where small herds of cattle and sheep grazed. They explored the orchards, canning house and outbuildings. Anna provided the history of the monastery and its meaning to the local community. She shared stories of her healing practice. Gertie and Sally interjected with stories of their own. The three young girls, once carefree in the parks of Berlin, had, by force and by choice, grown into amazing women.

On the second evening Sally's family and Matthew went into the village to experience the pub and mingle with the locals. They left the three women with uninterrupted time to share their stories.

"Gertie, I would like to hear more about your work." Sally wanted to hear more, and she wanted to learn more about her brother's remains and how Gertie came to possess them.

Gertie stood from her chair, paced in silence for a couple of minutes, then returned to their circle of chairs. She knelt before the women, taking a hand from each so they formed a circle. Gertie looked to the ground, then raised her face to look at the women. Her confident, accomplished aura was replaced with a meek, humble presence.

"In order to tell that story I have to share with you why my work evolved. I kneel here before you, begging you for acceptance and forgiveness as I share this story. You both deserve to hear it and I have to come clean for my own sanity."

"Come clean, Gertie? I'm sure..." Gertie stopped Sally.

"Yes, I have a very dark secret and I am going to share it with you now."

"Gertie, dear, get up off those old knees and take a seat before you start talking. I have lived in this house several decades. These walls have heard many confessions and I assure you that nobody has ever died from telling their story here."

"Thanks Anna. I'm not all too sure I can get back up if I stay like this the entire story." Gertie's mood lightened some as she released Sally and Anna's hands and grabbed the chair to pull herself up from the floor.

Gertie reminded the women of the photograph taken at the May pole dance in the park. She told them of the discovery, much later, that her father had orchestrated their families' presence at the festivities as part of the efforts to round up Jews. She went on to describe life with her mother, her stepfather, and her father's suicide.

"I had a lot of confusion early on. I hate to admit it but I did some things to survive that I am not proud of."

"You're being too hard on yourself, Gertie. You survived and look at all the good that has come from that. You really must forgive yourself." Anna attempted to console Gertie. Sally nodded in agreement.

"Yes, that's what my therapist said years ago and honestly, I think it took this reunion for me to find the right audience. There is nobody who would understand, or whose forgiveness and acceptance I need more than the two of you."

The three continued to talk about the war, the recovery of Berlin, the impact on them personally, and how their lives evolved because of their experiences. By the end of the evening, there was no doubt that Sally and Anna wholly accepted Gertie. Gertie retired that night feeling lighter, knowing that an enormous weight was lifted.

———

THE GUESTS EXTENDED their stay from overnight to three nights, but sadly the reunion came to an end. Sally and family planned to tour more of France before returning to the States where they would hold a memorial service for Isaac and bury his remains next to his mother. In the midst of the preparations to leave the monastery, Christopher came forward with a proposal that stunned all. He asked if he could stay on and study with Anna.

"I have found a teacher unlike any that I have previously studied with. Sister Anna has real world experience unlike any that I will have the honor of encountering in the future. My school does not start for another six weeks. I promise you this will be a life changing experience for me and I will be no trouble. I will help with the chores and study only as long as Sister Anna feels up to it so as not to tire her out."

Sister Anna stood by with a sheepish grin on her face. "Please, it was actually my idea that he stay on but I insisted that he ask for your permission first, before I affirmed. For many years I have prayed for one last student who could benefit from my experience and observations. I believe that prayer was answered with Christopher. I have received permission from Mother Superior and the Brothers have a vacant room in which he can stay. I do not mean to pressure but truly, as I have no biological children of my own, this would be my opportunity to pass on my legacy."

"We can see the importance to both of you. Christopher,

your father and I are so proud of you and Sister Anna, there is no better honor than to be invited to study with you." Christopher turned to his father, who slowly nodded in acceptance and agreement. "We will make arrangements for him to stay on with you but insist that if he tires you too much, you send him back home. We know how much energy he has."

Gertie, who rarely displayed emotion, sobbed in Sally's embrace. Without words, she felt forgiven and shed of a lifetime of self-doubt and shame.

EPILOGUE

The family stood outside airport security near the gate for Christopher's flight. Sally and Michael waved "welcome home Christopher" signs high above the crowd gathered there. Christopher spotted the sign, blushed slightly and quickened his pace to embrace his family.

"Oh Christopher, you look so wonderful, so mature." For the first time in her memory, Sally had not worried about Christopher during his adventure. She was confident when they left him with Anna that he was destined to have a wonderful experience.

"Thanks grandma. Thank you mom and dad for letting me stay. It was the most incredible experience. I want to tell you all about it, but I sure am hungry for a big old burger and fries. Can we please stop and get something to eat?" The family chuckled. His father ruffled his hair and arm in arm they traveled through the airport. They picked up his luggage and headed out in search of a burger and fries.

The group caught up over lunch and shared many laughs. Christopher shared stories of his studies with Sister Anna. He met several local villagers and enjoyed some extracurricular adventures with them.

The family separated after the meal to go their own directions. As Sally and George drove towards home, they reflected on the stories Christopher shared. He gained a lifetime of education and experience during the six weeks he stayed with Sister Anna at the monastery. He returned with the journals that Sister Anna recorded in for the many years she worked with patients. She helped Christopher set up his first journal using her system of observation. He had also been keeping journals of his discoveries, but found by using Sister Anna's method he brought more rigor and consistency to his observations.

"Grandma Sally, I really need to talk with you." Christopher had been home from his adventure in France for several months when he showed up at the front door of George and Sally's home.

"Honey, what is it? You look upset." Sally took his hand and pulled him inside. Christopher occasionally stopped by to visit them, but Sally sensed that this was an intentional visit.

"Can we sit down and have some tea?" Christopher wanted his grandmother to be comfortable when he shared today's news.

"Sure, sure. I'll heat the water. Your grandfather is out in the shop fixing a chair. Why don't you go out and ask him to join us too? I just made some butter cookies we can have with our tea."

The threesome sat around the kitchen table when the tea was ready. Christopher drew in a deep breath and took his grandmother's hand in his. "Grandma, I have some sad news from France. I got a call from the monastery. Our dear friend Anna passed away in her sleep yesterday." A tear slid down Christopher's face.

"Oh, my dear. I am so sad to hear this Christopher. Had she been ill?"

"Not really. Sister Louisa said she was very tired and napping a lot but had not missed mass or meals and her daily walk through the gardens. When I was with her, she told me that when she was much younger she had a vision in a dream. She knew from that dream that she would teach someone, a boy, about her healing work. She felt strongly that I was that boy and that her work on earth was fulfilled. I am not surprised to hear of her passing, but it does make me sad."

They sat silently for several minutes, taking in the news of Anna's passing and the implications of her dream.

"I have been so blessed to have met and worked with Anna and it's all because of you, grandma. I know you don't talk about your childhood much and it's really not fair for me to say this because I did not go through all that you went through but it seems much good has come from the terrible things you lived through. Anna said the same. You cannot image how thrilled she was to have a reunion with you and Gertie. She said that next to the work she did as God's hands, the reunion was the most important thing that had happened in her life. She talked about closing the circle of life and making sense of the lessons she had."

Sally dabbed her eyes with a tissue. "Christopher, you are a very keen young man. What you have witnessed many people, because their eyes are closed, have never seen in their lifetime. These are lessons that will shape your life in ways you may never know."

"Yes grandma, I believe that. I have been thinking about my life's work and I know that whatever I do, it will be an extension of all that I learned from Anna."

A few months later George and Sally met up with Gertie and Matthew in New York. They visited the gravesites of Isaac and Sally's mother. Gertie had aged significantly, and her stamina was low. Although in good spirits, her health was clearly failing. Within a year of their return to Australia, Gertie suffered a devastating stroke. Matthew cared for her at their home until finally, her heart rested eternally.

George and Sally frequently sat looking out of their enormous second-story window onto the gardens and forested area below. They spoke of their friends Anna, Gertie and Matthew with great fondness. While they were still living, they exchanged email, mail and telephone calls with them. Since Gertie's passing, Matthew had slowed down significantly and declined their invitations to visit them. "I'm content to be here at home, surrounded by the memories of Gertie. She still receives posthumous awards and recognition so I travel for that, but don't venture outside the country any longer."

"George, I am so thankful that you stuck with me. I know some of those years were very hard for you when I crawled into my shell and tried to make sense out of the life I was handed. You are a prince of a man and this beautiful home you built is such a blessing."

Their new home was warm with renewed passion and great joy of the life they shared despite the challenges they faced, separately and together.

George put his arm around her and pulled her so she rested on his chest. He, too, was grateful he had stayed on their path and witnessed the incredible becoming of his beautiful and talented wife.

As they reminisced, they often spoke of their grandsons who grew into fine young men. They carry with them legacies of love, loss and restoration. They watch Christopher's already fine character blossom as he displays compassion to others, and his studies intensified. Sally imagined her brother Isaac would have been of similar character had he survived the war. Anna's legacy truly lives on in Christopher, a stranger to her womb but kin to her heart.

ACKNOWLEDGMENTS

Writing a book is not a solo adventure. This book was developed through intuitive writing and meditation. I thank my editor and coach, Linda Zeppa, for all your encouragement and support in the process of writing this book.

I cannot thank my family enough for their support, enthusiasm, and patience. You tirelessly listened to my stories, witnessed the character development, and encouraged the completion of this project.

To Brenda, the patient and talented cover designer from Blue Valley Author Services, I thank you for helping me bring this book to life with a beautiful cover.

Angela, I appreciate your exceptional attention to detail in proofreading the manuscript.

For all those who inspire me through your stories, including those who have passed, thank you for your inspiration, your role modeling, and your perseverance as you faced all odds.

ABOUT THE AUTHOR

Kim Smart was raised in South Dakota, but *grew up* in Alaska after landing there as a young nurse. Two decades later, she moved to San Diego to attend law school. After graduating, she returned to Alaska to again work in health care, this time at the intersection with law and public health.

Kim has always had a diverse love for writing and reading, enjoying romance, women's literature, historical fiction, poetry, and stories of people living authentic lives. Following a lifelong dream, Kim has turned to writing. She currently writes romance, women's literature, and historical fiction, along with nonfiction articles for various publications.

When not writing or traveling, Kim enjoys time with her parents and extended family, hiking and creating in the kitchen. She presently lives in Arizona, or wherever the wind blows her as she visits her children, grandchildren, and other interesting parts of our world. She has much to write about and many stories to tell!

Join Kim to learn about new releases and exclusive reader giveaways. https://kimsmartauthor.com

ALSO BY KIM SMART

Buffalo Ridge Ranch Series

FALLING FOR HOME - BOOK 1

Jesse Davies was in love with his hometown girl for as long as he could remember. As they drift apart, he searches for meaning in his life. To find love, he must first find his voice and find himself.

Kerry Braun had dreams larger than Buffalo Ridge. To pursue those dreams, she leaves everything behind. The pursuit to become a veterinarian consumes her, blocking out all opportunities for lasting love. Will she ever find her way back?

Can two small-town friends find happily-ever-after?

TWO FOR LOVE - BOOK 2 (*Coming Spring 2020*)

Steve Davies lived his life in the shadow of his late wife's dreams. To emerge from his grief, he must take a chance. Hoping to expand the dreams they had together, he starts a dude ranch. In the process, he hires a cook - a city girl who brings along her son.

Bella Giordano needed to find safety for her young son. On a whim, she moves them from Manhattan to the Badlands of South Dakota, hoping the small town life, away from mob threats and smog, will be good for them both.

Will grief dissolve and a new opportunity be enough to build a new family?

The second novel in Kim Smart's Buffalo Ridge Ranch series sets the table for new opportunities and the possibility of love. Will hurts heal and love grow?

Chance Davies, champion bull rider, goes from being rock star of the rodeo to broken and lost after a final ride turns into a tragic accident. He is forced to return to Buffalo Ridge Ranch for recuperation after many years on the circuit. Through hard work and challenging himself, his body starts to heal. But will he allow his mind and spirit to heal and open up to new opportunities?

Sheltered from love, Pauline Whyte was always a misfit in the small town of Buffalo Ridge where everyone knew her family's business. She escaped the town gossip for a few years by moving away, only to have to return to care for her ailing father. Somehow, in this small town, love finds its way to her. Can she accept it?

To let love in, they must overcome loss and pain. Will her misfit ways fit into his new life for a happily-ever-after?

The third novel in Kim Smart's Buffalo Ridge Ranch series brings a story of overcoming the odds. Is that enough to find true love?

Stella Davies lived far away from Buffalo Ridge Ranch. Fearing repeat abandonment, she built the life of a cowboy nurturing her herd on the rugged edge of nature in Arizona. But to find happiness, she must face these fears. When she moves to the remote high desert, she is forced to face her fears.

Ranching was in Brandon Cage's blood, but a new career as a lawyer changed his focus. He buried himself in his new profession and totally ignored his heart's desires.

Do they have the gumption to clear the way to give love a chance? Will their love arrive in time to find a life happily-ever-after?

The fourth novel in Kim Smart's Buffalo Ridge Ranch series is about overcoming past hurts and prioritizing love.